WAHEIGI LEITENG

ꯋꯥꯍꯩꯒꯤ ꯂꯩꯇꯦꯡ

Garland of Words

PRADIUM MOIRANGTHEM

BlueRoseONE
Stories Matter
New Delhi • London

BLUEROSE PUBLISHERS
India | U.K.

For permissions requests or inquiries regarding this publication, please contact:

BLUEROSE PUBLISHERS
www.BlueRoseONE.com
info@bluerosepublishers.com
+91 8882 898 898
+4407342408967

ISBN: 978-93-7542-880-0

Cover design: Ajay
Typesetting: Manisha Rawat

First Edition: February 2026

Acknowledgements

I would like to thank Oinam Chingkheinganba for bringing positivity in my life. Chingkheinganba, whom I call him Chingkhei, came to my life as a beacon of hope when I was in my dark phase. Thank you Chingkhei!

I am thankful to my father Moirangthem Saratchandra Singh for his presence in my life. My father has been realistic in giving advice, helpful and at times harsh with words, and it helped me in setting my priorities in life. Yes, I admit, I do keep secrets from him, but he is also my best friend.

I would like to thank Potsangbam Saroja Devi, my cousin and best friend, who has been my strong pillar in my life. Her presence in my life provide me with a positive impact in my life.

I would like to thank Laishram Samson Singh, who plays an important role in my life as a very supportive senior. I am grateful to have him in my life.

I am thankful to Moirangthem Winner for being a supportive elder brother.

I am thankful to Chanamthabam Ronika, Oyam Litin, Munmun Debnath, Shravana Rajkumari, Leimapokpam Nancy Chanu, Dudu for their tremendous support in my life.

Lastly, I would like to thank all my well wishers for their support and help in this journey.

Contents

Chapter 1: Airport Memories, diary entries, and life! 1

Chapter 2: Is this even possible? 44

Chapter 3: The Blue Lotus 57

Chapter 4: The Final High School Year 73

Chapter 5: Papa, bless me with a happily ever after! 86

Chapter 1

Airport Memories, diary entries, and life!

Airport! Airport! Airport! It's a place where in Bollywood, Hero meets the Heroine and end up with a happily ever after post-credit scenes, a place where near and dear ones come to say goodbye, and a place where people meet after a long gap. And for me, it has been a place where my father, and elder brother would wait for me. It's a place where the goodbye is harsh. It's a place where I shouted at Patrick, cursed him, expected him to console me. It's also a place where I met Lamnganba, and I got motivated to write this book.

I have been thinking quite long enough to write a book on my high school memories- Maria Montessori School, or I should say, Maria Montessori Senior Secondary School, Imphal as was called during my time, a decade earlier. I have so many memories with this school. From the Basketball court, to the football ground, to the Physics Lab, Burgeon Block, Welkin Block and Genesis Block, this school has given me so many memories. Even after 09 years of completion of my High School life, I am connected to my school in some way, through my classmates, seniors, juniors, teachers and connecting with them make me relive those moments again.

I am presently sitting in Indigo 6E958, seat 17A, facing the laptop screen, enroute to Bengaluru from Kolkata. It's 4:21 PM IST, and as I see from the window, I can see white blanket of clouds of fog. There is sky blue colour above the horizon. The buzzing of the air turbine boasts me of it's scientific accuracy. It's amazing to know that I am living my moment in an Aeroplane, about 10,000 feets above the Ground and travelling back to Bengaluru. I won't say it's cloudy, rather I will say that it's hazy.

It was at 8:40 AM when Lamnganba called me. I missed his call. I texted him, "Hi Lamnganba, I am not able to pick your call at the moment. Is there anything?"

"Can I drop you to the Airport?" He asked.

"I will need to ask Papa. He is also getting ready to drop me off to the Airport."

"No worries da Arun, I can come to the Airport instead."

I did call Lamnganba in the morning. I had published a Manipuri novel named Ashangba Thambal, and I got ten author copies. I wanted to give one of the copies to him. He didn't pick the call when I was standing at the front of his house to give one of the copies. He called me a while later, but I had already went to distribute my book to Natasha, and other friends.

Papa dropped me to the Airport. And, Lamnganba was there, waiting for me. He wore a formal shirt and a formal pant, with well polished dark tan shoes. His white shirt has designs and motifs of black ink. He had a sunglass on his pocket as well. He looked really good, a combination of poised gentleman and masculine physique.

I waved a hi at him as soon as I got down from my XUV 500. I smiled at him. I felt a sudden sense of gratitude because he waited for me at the airport. It's so rare for me. My boyfriend does wait for me at the Airport but it is hardly voluntary. What Lamnganba did was voluntary, and I felt respected, seen and valued. "Thank you Lamnganba," I told myself.

Some people come in your life for a few moments and create of wave of positive change in your life. Today, it has been Lamnganba. He gave me a bunch full of hope and positivity. We talked for a while. Papa had gone for an Ushop, which consists of offering prayers, followed by eating the food offering, which comprises of rice, varieties of lentils, vegetables, paneer, as part of the ritual.

In front of the seats placed before the Departure Gate, we sat for a while.

"Da Malemnganba is getting married this January," he said.

"Time flies, doesn't it? My school senior who was about 17 when I first met him is getting married next year," I told myself.

I smiled at him and said, "This is indeed a very happy news."

When I talk about airport memories, I tend to get flashbacks about da Malemnganba and da Patrick. I once dropped da Malemnganba to the Airport, along with da Lamjingba, and that is a different story I will tell later.

My alma mater turns 40 this year. I could not resist myself to write about my school. Maria Montessori School, Imphal has given me alot. From friendships, hope, my first crush, I can say that I had a unique experience. I have lost touch with many of my classmates, but those handful, with whom I am still in contacts with, have been a very strong support in my life. I see whatsapp stories of my classmates once in a while, and that's how I am connected to most of them. Some have become gym freaks, some are preparing for exams, some have got married, and here I am, writing books and working at the same time. Everyone is busy with their life.

I loved writing since my school days. I felt very happy when I received a certificate of Appreciation for my contribution as a member of the Literary Club, Maria Montessori Senior Secondary School, Imphal. That certificate, with blue colour border, along with the logo of my school, was so precious to me. And I finally earned it. I have to be honest here. I took part in Shot Put competition, poetry competition, and I lost. Losing in these competitions did make way for me to work harder.

English has always scared me. I would get relatively higher marks in all the other subjects, but when it came to English, I would hardly secure 60 out of 100. Things did change in the XII Board Exam results. I ended up being the fourth position holder for the Batch of 2016. You will find the name of Arthur Kangjam on the School Topper Honour Board, Loitongbam Natasha Chanu on the Physics, Chemistry, Biology Subject Topper Honour Boards. You will not find my name in any of the Honour Boards, but I live in the names of my schoolmates. I live on in the memories of my schoolmates. A boy who was 15 joins a new school, falls in love with a school senior. I miss myself being a teenager again. I have been so innocent back then. Looking back, I want to hug my younger self and say, "Arun, I am proud of you. You are carrying yourself really well. You must be doubting yourself, but trust me, you did well in life."

Isn't it surprising that I have decided to write a story based on my school life? That too after nearly a decade. I did try writing a fiction story based on my school life. But then, I got writer's block and that story collapsed mid-way. I was also scared whether I could do justice writing about my school. Then now, where is this energy coming from? It's personal because there is very less time left and I want to gift this book to my senior.

November 16 has always been an auspicious day for me. I have so many memories with respect to this particular day. It was on this particular day, November 16, 2014 when I saw my senior Okram Malemnganba receive Chairman's Award for Leadership. I was among the audience that day, and I remember that moment very clearly. One year later, I participated Khamba-Thoibi Dance (or Lai Haraoba Dance) as a part of a cultural program by Class XII students. There again, I met da Malemnganba receiving the award of being the topper of the Batch.

From my batch, it was Arthur Kangjam. Ever since Arthur joined the school, he has been the school topper. I did feel happy when I met him for the first time. He was a position holder in his previous school as well. He came from Board of Secondary Education, Manipur and he did well in Central Board of Secondary Education as well.

I had always been connected to the school in one way or the other. My cousins Nongdren and Leima would tell me about the 25th Foundation Day Celebration. "It was a grand event," che Leima would say. She was two class senior to me. So, when I was in Class IX, she was in Class XI. It was in Class IX when I tried getting admission to Maria Montessori School. But, there was no opening for students to get admitted in Class IX. I didn't want to repeat Class VIII again, so I waited two more years and appeared in the entrance exams for new admissions of Class XI students.

My cousin Leima guided me about the tuitions. I used to go to Sir Kamal's tuition, who was a Marian teacher. And, I was surrounded by many Marians since then. So, when I cleared the entrance exam and got admitted to this school in Class XI, it didn't feel as if I am a new comer.

I remember my first day at school. I waited for the bus, Kamakhya Travels was the bus name. And Ma'am Rita was our bus-in-charge. I loved my day. At the basketball court, there was a notice board showing our sections – A, B, C, and D.

Initially, Calvin was in section D, but he had opted for Manipuri, so he got shifted to Section A. Section D was a mix of newcomers and oldcomers. It was such a beautiful mix because it was unique in it's own way. Newcomers brought their own personalities and it synced with the oldcomers, though initially some face offs was observed. It all got better in the end. I had been told by some of my classmates that in Class IX as well, the shuffling of section happened.

A new block named Welkin block was newly inaugrated. And, it was for Class XI and Class XII students. I didn't have a good command in English when I was in Class XI. My appearance was I was overweight, I had a stooped over spine posture, sign of an underconfident person. And I will not say that I was ever confident during my entire school life. Except for that one event when I reminded myself of che Rajeswari Chongtham, and it gave me the courage to speak up in the assembly.

Ma'am Director told once in the assembly, "If you can become a leader, be a good leader. And if you cannot become a leader, be a good follower, but choose your leader wisely."

I closed my eyes and I saw da Lamjingba, da Malemnganba, and da Nelson. That's when I decided that I will follow them. Whenever I was in doubt with my life, I would ask myself, "What would da Lamjingba, da Malemnganba, and da Nelson collectively do, if they were in this situation?" And it helped me.

I loved dancing. I had been dancing since Class V, in my previous schools. I would take part in cultural dance programmes. And it made me happy. I had lost touch in dance after I started class IX, as there were bunch of tuition classes waiting for me before and after school. But in class XII, things did change. I took part in the Khamba-Thoibi dance. About 50 students took part in the dance. That day I met da Meiramnganba again, to receive the school topper award for the year 2024. Physics, Chemistry, Biology honour boards had his name too. And I was a proud witness when his name was written. In Chemistry, da Sudhakar Athokpam was also given the school subject topper award.

I have one more habit. I never received a rank. I would pass all the subjects but never made it to the top 10. But things changed in Class XII board exams. I gave my best and secured fourth position with 89.8%. I was short of one mark to secure 90%. It is funny because I used to joke around saying, "let's aim for 90%," whenever I met my classmates.

I was not good in sports, but I took part in a health run 5km. I was also a participant in poetry. I didn't win any of these in Class XI. But in Class XII, I got something, I got fifth position in the State Level Essay Writing competition by Manipur Biodiversity Board. In the school level, there was an essay writing competition. I was among the two selected to represent my school. The other was my classmate, George Konsam.

Looking back, it fills me with pride that I am a part of Maria Montessori School, Imphal. As a Marian, I do follow the motto: deeds not words, as much as I can. I am fortunate enough to receive education in this esteemed school because the school was liberal. The school was liberal to students belonging to the LGBTQ+ community. I, who identify as gay, was not courageous enough to live by my identity. And, as I write this, there is still fear inside of me. And I think it will always be there, though I am able to minimize this fear with each passing day. The fear of humiliation, shame, guilt, disgust still chills my spine. I was not financially independent, I was scared about my parents' reaction, I was scared about my father's reaction. To be honest, as I am writing this, I am still concerned about my father's probable reaction.

What will the society say? What will my boyfriend's family say? My boyfriend is not ready to publicly declare our relationship. And that's why I changed his name, as Patrick. Patrick is the name of a character from a series named Schitt's Creek. My boyfriend adores this character. He once said, "I want a Patrick in my life." And I want to tell him, "But dear boyfriend, we are born in India, and I feel that you have given up on this relationship." I am nowhere near the Schitt's Creek Patrick's personality, but yes, I do try to be my best version for him.

Habits are what defines us in the long run. It is the base of our character. If I do negative and less productive habits, I will be defined as a negative and less productive person. I try to indulge in neutral and positive habits, which aligns with my future goals and well-being. I try to include gym, proper sleep schedule, dance, sketch, study for exams, and becoming a better person each day. The only pain I have is my boyfriend's reaction. He has become distant from me. There are days when I just want to give up and sit quietly on a sofa, but that's okay as well. It is a natural reaction to be sad when your lover doesn't text you back. Everyone of us have ups and downs in their lives, it's how we deal with each of these emotions.

I am happy that I have many goals. One of the goal is to complete this manuscript. I want to contribute to the Indian literature as much as I can by writing novels, novellas, short stories, and poems. I got the urge to learn Meitei Mayek script when I was in Class XI. I wanted to read what my fellow Marians were writing in Manipuri on the annual magazine. I learnt English and Hindi in my previous schools. I never got the opportunity to learn Manipuri at school. It was during my college days when I decided to learn the Meitei Mayek script. Over time, I knew how to type in Meitei Mayek, and it became my new skill.

I realised that I am good at learning languages. I am presently learning Kannada. Life is an ever-evolving process, where we can learn along the way. I have exams, I have many goals in life. I learnt that career, mental and physical health is as much important as love life. I have invested so much for my lover, yet I feel it's not enough to make him closer to me. And I realised that I should preserve my energy and invest on myself, my dreams, my goals, my deepest wishes. Patrick is important, no doubt, but I am important as well.

"Your boyfriend is an unemphatetic person," Mala said on the phone. She is my childhood friend, since Class V. She is not wrong. He has not texted me a single text since two days. And, he can still survive. Maybe I have been giving him so many chances and got blind in love that I didn't see his toxic side. He is the same with his parents too. He will seldom call his parents. And, that means, he is an emotionally less available person. How am I supposed to spend a lifetime with an emotionally less available person? Okay, let's still accept this trait of his, but what about his responsibility in this relationship? Why would he do this to me?

These are questions I ask myself. And I am concerned about my father too. I wish to say, "Dear Papa, it is hard for me to explain this to you. I am not sure how you will take this. But I am in love with a man. And I am a gay man, and I have no shame in stating my sexual identity. I cannot live a fake life." I am not ready to talk to my father about this. Likewise, I feel that Patrick is not ready to live this open, out of the closet life. He is still fighting with himself. He talks to himself, "Why am I gay? Why am I born this way? If I was born straight, all of my life problems would have been solved." I feel bad for him. And I have started to feel that we are not compatible anymore. It has started to feel that it was only me who was in the relationship. And he is not even trying to make this relationship work. Like an old Lion in the jungle awaiting for his last breath, he has given up on his life. But, life cannot be lived on auto-pilot all the time. One has to take actions towards his chosen goals. I feel that living with me is not his priority for the moment. And, he is even ready to give up on this relationship. I want to punch him on his face, so badly. But I love him as well.

Let me explain more elaborately. I got attracted to him because he reminds me of my toxic traits. I do see possibility of him getting better over time. But, what truly attracts me to him is his attitude. He is emotionally less available, and it gives me a rush to chase for him. He blames himself for his sexual orientation. I also blame myself for my sexual orientation as well, but not much as him. And I regret blaming myself. He is going through a lot, and it feels good to be around him. And that is why I am still clinging on to him, no matter what.

Office lunch time is usually my time when I read some novels and write some sentences. But for now, it's all about thinking about Patrick. Why is Patrick acting this way? Why is he being distant from me? Maybe I should also stop talking to him. Let's see! I should focus on my other aspects of life. I should focus on myself and do the needful. That way, I can be happy. Patrick needs space, and I am not able to give him space. I also need to tell my subconscious self that nothing will happen even if Patrick is not in my life. Anyways, he is very absent from my life. He isn't concerned whether I am surviving or not, because he is not able to take care of himself. Will he cry if I die? He might, but what's the use of crying after I am dead. He should make me happy when I am alive. I should not keep my life revolving around Patrick. I have decided that I will not be initiate talking to Patrick. Just 14 days!

I have a book to write. I have a whole syllabus to complete. I must not keep myself entangled in love. This love feeling has to go, since it is causing me anxiety. I will decide on 21/12/2025. Till then, I will be focussed on all other aspects of life. Health – physical and mental, career – present and future, hobbies – writing, reading, Kannada, sketch, digital art, acrylic art, and many more.

I requested Natasha to help me in this process. She readily agreed. She said, "You can call me at 10:00 PM everyday and we will discuss what you are feeling." And, I write on the diary gifted by her.

05/12/2025

Dear Natasha,

I have decided that I will not be initiating conversation with Patrick till 19/12/2025. Fourteen days it is, many things can happen in these fourteen days. Maybe we can come more closer. Alternatively, it can go complete opposite. I am scared. My liver has come to my throat. Haha! I know it doesn't make any sense. A liver never comes to the throat. I wanted to express that my heart fears that we will break up sooner or later. And the way he is treating me, responding to my calls, texts, I myself feel ashamed of myself. He ignores me. And here I am, writing about him, to you. Why does he say, "Change my name while you write about me." Why does he say, "Don't write my name on acknowledgements." His mother disgusts our relationship. I dislike her too. But why is he like that? He is torn between his sexual identity and family. And I am also bearing the pain he is going through. It is hard for me to not talk to him, so I am venting my emotions here, for fourteen days. Okay then, I will not approach him for fourteen days, and let me see where this relationship goes. I do love him, there's no doubt. But it's time to live for myself a little more. A bare minimum effort to myself, while giving the utmost attention to him is not working. I realised it late, but I am glad I realised it. So, no Patrick for the coming 14 days. It is a challenge to myself to show that I can survive without Patrick for fourteen days.

Yours,
Arun
13 December 2025, Saturday 02:00AM

Dear Natasha,

I have finally comes to terms that I can be happy, with or without Patrick. He has finally been taken down from the pedestal of boyfriend. I have nearly no expectations from him anymore. I want to be the old Arun who was serious about academics, novels and life. I have finally recovered from my grief phase. I cry at times, but my tears have dried up now. Patrick, I let you be yourself. I understand that you are going through alot, and your brain is not working. Your mom's and dad's deteriorating health, your unacceptance of your identity, your innate nature of being emotionally unavailable are all factors that are surrounding you at the moment. I would have loved if you had shared about your day. I would have appreciated if you had showed interest in my life. But now, I am over it. I know that you will never ask me about my day, whether I have eaten or not, or whether I have done anything wonderful. But, why do I need to wait for him to ask me? I don't need his permission to share him about my day, and ask about my day. He is independent. Likewise, I am independent too. We don't have any ground rules too. He is being himself and I am being myself.

I choose to take care of myself. I choose to be happy. I choose to focus on things which are in my control. I choose to be disciplined, focussed on my physical and mental health. I promise myself that I will be my best version this moment onwards.

Life's hard at the moment. The job needs me. Back to back night casting is happening and that's hard. I want to challenge myself. Can I crack RRB JE? Can I crack GATE 2026? Can I crack ESE 2026? It's all something that time, hardwork and dedication will decide.

I choose to be proactive. I choose to be working on myself and achieving mroe than I could achieve with average efforts. I have finally got the kick inside me. I have got ambitious to be fit, an achiever in work life, one who can make as much time for hobbies. I must work towards my well-being.

How can I live a fulfilling life? I can live a fulfilling life by focussing on my career, working on my hobbies, taking care of my health, removing stress from my life. Patrick gives me stress and it's for my best that I remove him from the centre of my life. I have stopped connecting with him as much as possible. It doesn't hurt anymore too. I have realised that I can be happy with or without him. I should not worry about my future, where things are beyond my control. I can focus on the present and work on targets which I prefer as outcomes in my future.

For example, if I want to be a good author, I must write and read now. If I want a lean fit physique, I must focus on calorie-deficit diet and exercise. If I want to be a good engineer, I must focus on being a good MCQ solver, and a skilled engineer. And if I want Patrick in my life, I must let him be, distance myself from him to keep my sanity, and be my best version. It is on him to either stay or not stay with me. I cannot force him. I can only provide him with an information that I am available in his life. This change in thought reduces a lot of stress. I am no longer stressful, now that I have come in terms and accepted Patrick the way he is. Loving him is a choice. Leaving him is also a choice. I choose to love him, and myself too. For the sake of my happy and healthy well-being, I let Patrick be himself. I no longer expect texts or calls from him. I don't expect him to send me Good Morning texts, caring words. I have also made sure that he shouldn't expect devotion from me anymore. As and when I realise that he is a waste of my effort, time and energy, I will leave him for the better. That's all Natasha.

Yours,
Arun
December 13, 2025 Saturday 08:40 PM

Dear Natasha,

I think I have realised the fact that Patrick is an emotionally unavailable person. I don't feel important in this relationship. And, it is best for me to realise that he has hurt me. I need to respect myself and my time. he didn't talk to me the whole day. I don't blame him but I have realised that I should end this relationship. It's not his mom's opinions, Gunachandra's, or other peoples' opinions, it's that his behaviour is not compatible with me anymore. Earlier, I used to chase him, but now, I have stopped chasing him. I have realised that it's time to let go. I have realised that it's time to choose myself.

Why should I be bothered about him, care about him, when he cannot do the same? One shouldn't be in a relationship if he/she cannot provide time for a partner in a day. He has the ability to survive without texting me. This is the end. I am ending this relationship. I am sorry that I bring up this topic everytime. All I can say is that I have finally moved on from him. It did hurt but it doesn't hurt anymore.

I don't believe that he will change anymore in his life. I wish him the best. I wish myself the best. We are no longer compatible. Thanks to my clinical psychologist Dr Geeta's advice to not reach out to him, now I have realised that he was barely available in the relationship. That's all. He needs to grade up, and I need to move on.

Civil engineering, dance, sketch, gym, diet and proper sleep is what is needed. Of course I need to learn Kannada. I aspire to be a Kannada writer too. Patrick and I are no longer together. This is the closure. I give the closure. I blame his emotionally unavailable nature. From today, I have promised myself that I will not be together with him. This is it. One week of talking to you, and realising that I must leave him, for my life growth, soul nourishment, and betterment of my life. Enough crying for him.

I am gay. I am a civil engineer. I am an emotionally available, caring boyfriend. I am a dancer. I am an artist. I am Mr Gay India 2025 first runner up. And, I can break up with Patrick because he hurt me, has been emotionally unavailable, abandoned me, made me cry, made me feel less worthy, treated me badly. Why should I make myself feel disrespected, feel less about myself? Why should I continue to give time for him, when all he can do is ignore me, disrespect me, get irritated by me? I, consciously decide to break up with him. I am happier now.

Fine, let me focus on civil engineering, writing, sketch, gym, Kannada, meditation. NO Patrick from today. 21/12/2025 will be my last time I will see him. This is the end. Goodbye. I will focus on myself from now on. That's all. He chose his mom's words over me. He chose his homophobic best friend Gunachandra over me. He chose to be emotionally unavailable, go silent on me, and I should never forget that. I forgive him and I have also awarded myself with self-love, more time, and energy.

Yes, I am sexually attracted to him. His voice attracts me, but I should also not forget his shortcomings. He is not a husband material. He will not keep me happy. Otherwise, I would have always been happy. I am not happy at the moment, and it is because of his emotionally unavailable nature. It does hurt to end a future with him. But, he doesn't convince me. He doesn't give me assurance that I will have a happy, fulfilling future with him.

There are good moments – Mr Gay India 2025 pageant, our live in, the way he confronted his mom, but that's not enough to compensate for his silent behaviour. I want a partner who cares for me, is a good friend, loves me, doesn't hurt me, shows efforts, is available, is confident enough to introduce me to his friends. And, I must also look for a caring second family. This is it. I end this relationship.

I will be a good civil engineer, writer, get into a fit physique, and a Kannada, Tamil and Telugu writer. That's all.

I need to complete the novel : 'Waheigi Leiteng' The Garland of Words.

Malemnganba, my school senior, who has been my Hero in school life. I have his photo cut and pasted on my diary of 2015. I also pasted a newspaper clipping where my school congratulated him for his selection in the Indian Army. It was a beautiful and proud thing to have met him. It was beautiful to have witnessed him in my life. I smile when I see him. I smile when I think about him. I don't have money to go to Imphal for his marriage. I will not be able to meet him if I don't go to his wedding. I want to witness his marriage. But presently, I have financial constraints. I have not booked tickets too. It's okay to invest my money and go to his wedding. But, I also need to consider about money. I need to be financially aware of my decisions. I must consider my life to be in a balance. Writing a book about him is also a blessing, and gratitude. I must understand that I need to take control of my life. Financially, spiritually, mentally, physically, emotionally, I should take the best decision. Only then I can achieve good things in life.

Garland of words,

I devote to you.

May you achieve everything in your life,

May you be your best version.

You have done well in your life,

You have made our school proud.

I am proud of you,

I am grateful to you too.

Make your way to glory,

For I believe in you.

Dedicated to da Malemnganba, da Lamjingba, Natasha and all fellow Marians who have outdone their average versions in their life.

Life is about taking risks. Life is about striving for the better. Life is about becoming our better version. Life is about living. Life is about being happy. Life is about taking care of oneself. Life is about loving oneself to the extent that one makes circumstances where one is respected and valued. I must be a resourceful person. I should be my best version.

I have finally decided to love myself. I found myself and I will work to upgrade my life.

Yours,
Arun
15 December 2025, Monday

Dear Natasha,

I am sorry I lied to you. I did talk with Patrick. It does hurt when a person you love doesn't love you back. You have been calling me every 10:00 PM since 6/12/2025 to ask how I am doing in my life. As agreed, we will be discussing till 20/12/2025 whether I should have Patrick in my life or not. The thing is, Patrick is not the problem. The problem is my time mismanagement. Good thing is amidst all this chaos, I am able to write about Patrick. That's also a good thing. I am self analysing myself. Thank you for your time. I have realised that he doesn't prioritise me as much as I prioritise him. I am no perfect boyfriend, and I have done things which clearly states that I should move away from this relationship. I slept with a man yesterday. I admit that it was for temporary pleasure, and that's a reason enough that I should separate from Patrick.

Patrick and I don't share anything anymore. And, in a way, I must say that I should stop actively searching for a partner. It is hard to end this relationship. Looking at the circumstances, it's hard for me to decide. I will not blame him. It's my fault too. I am not a loyal boyfriend. I seeked pleasure from other men. I am not sure whether I should be indifferent about this. Should I be ashamed to admit that I have multiple sex partners? I do love Patrick. His silence hurts me. His emotional unavailability hurts me. And I think he doesn't want me in his life anymore.

Our conversations are getting painfully quieter. I am not sure whether I am healing or in pain. I am sexually attracted to him. I love him. Sex is a very important driving force and I know that I am very much into him. I cannot just resist him. He is addictive. The point is I am not able to love him unconditionally. He hurts me but I love him so much.

I will meet him on 21/12/2025. I will choose him no matter what. It's better that I change my attitude towards him and treat him with respect. Things will get better with him. I can always choose to love him. But I must also not forget that I have a career to make.

All I can say is, "Dear Natasha, I want to be a better boyfriend, a better civil engineer, a better writer, a better artist, a better dancer, a better human."

I will save this relationship, come what may. I will change myself. I will speak less. I will be the man that Patrick wants me to be. I will protect him from the world. I have so much expectations from him. I cannot stop loving him. But yes, till 20/12/2025, I will give him the break. He deserves all the love and respect. I shouldn't forget that.

Five days will slip by in the blink of an eye. I am not sure what will happen, but I can surely navigate this love boat in the favour of our relationship. That being said, I have an entire syllabus in front of me. I have barely started. Let me stop talking to him for five days and let him decide if he wants to be in a relationship with me or not. I decide that I will keep the relationship alive, but it should be his call too. He is too precious to be lost. He is my diamond. I cannot bargain him with anything.

I am sorry that I got angry at Patrick. I am not happy, I wanted to show him that. But, I want him to be happy. I will be happy. Christmas is coming, my birthday is coming, four year anniversary with him is coming. He will always be mine. I cannot live without him.

I forgive myself for sleeping with other men. I forgive myself for being an insecure man in the relationship. I forgive myself for using dating apps, for being immature and for all my behaviour I think is unproductive, bad and unhealthy.

I need to grow up. I am Patrick's and Patrick is mine. This is all I should know. I think Natasha I am sorted now.

All I need is love, respect, career stability, happiness and hope. I must take care of myself. This human life is just very precious.

What's the point if I cannot bring stability in a relationship? What's the point if I cannot respect myself? What's the point if I cannot do what I love?

I love writing, reading, dancing, sketch, solving numericals. I must take care of myself and respect him.

Yours,
Arun

What's the difference between love and attachment? What's the difference between one-sided love and two-sided love? For me, I am in love with Patrick. He has stolen my heart, my soul and I cannot live without him. I want to text him, call him everyday. It's hard for me when he doesn't reciprocate my love. It has come to my notice that he has lost interest in me. He doesn't talk to me properly. He is supposed to come to Bengaluru on 21st December, 2025. He texted me on whatsapp, "Don't come to meet me on 21 Dec, I want to spend time alone."

"Let God give me the courage to break your TV if you come on 21 December. Stay at a Hotel, I will be locking the house door." I was angry and I shouldn't have said things which I said anyway.

He is also no less in arguments. He replied back, "Who do you think you are?"

I didn't cry. He has very less to say, and he said this. Fine, I have decided that I will take care of myself, get busy, love him, avoid contacts with him till 21/12/2025. It's so funny that I always hope things will work out with him. Love is dead, it's the attachment which is left. From my end, love is there. From his end, I am not sure if he still wants to continue this relationship. I need to take care of myself, let him be for a while, but how do I tell myself that he shouldn't exist in my life.

I cannot give up on this relationship. He is toxic to me, I feel. But I love him and it has blinded me to not see his shortcomings. Will I ever find someone like him again? Will I ever be happy being single? I have been in a relationship for nearly four years and I feel that this is the longest time where he has been acting differently. Will he come back to me? Will he stand by me? In the present scenario, he is someone who wishes to escape from this relationship. He wants to be alone. I think I should let him be. My angry version wants to end this relationship. My caring version wants to save this relationship. He is avoidant, I am anxious, and both of us are toxic to each other. I think that in the push and pull of this relationship, I have stopped being a friend to him. A friend cares. A friend accepts the flaws of a friend. A friend listens to a friend. I think I need to take a break, and give him a break to process things. I must stay silent till 20/12/2025. No words, no sentences, no connection. Let's see if he can also be silent. I believe he can stay silent. I am worried about me. This break is really important for me. I wish if he becomes a caring boyfriend who texts me, calls me, cares for me.

This is not the end. Also, I am not just a lover boy. I have other aspects too. I need to take care of my health and be conscious where I give my time to. He is hurting. I shouldn't hurt him more. Let his wounds heal on his own till 20/12/2025. Let him be happy. I love him.

Dear Natasha,

The funny thing about me is I am not giving up on this relationship. I like chasing him. I like annoying him. This is all acceptable to an extent, but there is also a limit. I cannot just focus on him. I do also have a life – my career as a civil engineer, my goals to be a lean fit person, my goals to be a good writer, good dancer, good artist, and my hobby to learn Kannada. I need to divide my time in such a way that even during my crisis with Patrick, I have a safe space to clear my mind, by getting busy in doing things, which will help me in the future. It can be either through upskilling myself, indulging in my hobbies, taking care of myself by not doing unproductive habits. Unproductive habits are those habits which don't really help me in my present or future. These are short term pleasures, with a lot of drawbacks and consequences later in life.

Natasha, I want to be a better person. Do you remember a time in Class XII, where I was crying? I cried during the Foundation Week 2015. I nominated myself for the Shot Put competition, and I lost in the sport. Two students were selected from each house, I was from Einstein House. I secured sixth position out of the eighth. I could have nominated someone better than me. I lost a medal and also a vacancy. I cried that day because I remembered da Lamjingba who won a Silver Medal for the same sport.

It was you who asked me, "What happened Arun?"

I did tell you the story. Looking back, I realise that it's no big deal. But as a sixteen year old, it was a big deal. Wow! I am a decade older now. I miss my teenage version, who did well in his studies, got a mild crush on his school senior Lamjingba, and was dealing with his sexual orientation. Adolescense is in itself a very complex thing, so many changes occur. Merely describing it as biological and physical changes are not enough to express what I went through that time. But I am happy now.

School got over. College life began. And after that, I am working now. Life changed alot in a decade. I should say that the effort I put in my Class XII, I never put that effort ever again. I think I did put effort on my love life, but not on my studies. I have been putting average efforts in everything. Maybe even in writing, sketch, dance, living my life. How do I change this? I know that if I give my best effort in my career, I can do well in life. But that's not entirely true as well? With my present capacity, time, money and resources, I am doing decently good. But, one should also aspire to get better in life. It should not become stagnant.

That's a good thing to realise. Dear Natasha, it's hard to live a life where my boyfriend has gone silent. It's hard to focus on other things in life. But I have to focus. I have to focus on my career, I have to focus on my life. I am not that sad like before. I am better now. I am no longer a cry baby for Patrick. But, I don't want to end my relationship with him too. That's hope.

That being said, I am still living my life. I am doing good in my office work. I am writing everyday. Yes, exam preparation is not going that well. I should say, the exam preparation is not going well at all. Maybe I should divert my focus on career now. Patrick may stay or may not stay. My main focus for now is my career. I must work on my career. And I will do the needful.

There's a saying that goes, "One does great things when one has a plan and less time." I think this is what motivated me to write. I have less time, and it has motivated me to complete this novel. It is indeed very tiring to exist in this so called night duty. I am tired. I feel sleepy and I am in no shape to focus on myself at the moment. I cannot concentrate. I am so confused because I have books to read, prepare for exams, complete writing a manuscript, go to the gym, learn Kannada. I have so many things lined up and I am not able to focus on anything at all. This hurts me because I am not able to focus on more important things in life.

All I can say is I am tired. I have night duty and I am sitting in front of my laptop and sharing what I am feeling at the moment. It's 00:41 AM and I am tired. I have lost concentration. But I am happy also because I am able to control my bad habits. And, I am able to focus on my other aspects of my life, such as civil engineering, writing and gym.

Life's hard. I made one thing in life. I made Patrick as my centre of my life. But right now, I am not able to concentrate on other aspects of life. I have realised that I should not revolve my life around him. I have dreams to accomplish. I have a life to make, and I have very less time. Actually, I do have time. It's just that I am focussing on the little time I have left, on my own set deadline. And the fact is, I can still focus on my work and beautify my work, make it more better and do the best I can. This is important.

Secondly, I must learn from my mistakes. I cannot make the same mistakes again and again. And, this is what I realised with time. Maybe that's what being an adult is. We make mistakes, we learn from them and decide whether we should repeat them or not. Is Patrick a mistake? I don't know. But he is important. He is important because I have many happy memories with him. And I want to keep him in my life. He seems directionless at the moment. He seems confused with his life. He seems sad and I feel he also makes me more sad. I am there to help him but he doesn't give me the space to help him.

Deeds not words. I should apply this in my love life too. I decide to love him, with as much less expectations as I can. I decide to focus on my goals, of being a writer, and a dancer, a good civil engineer, a physically fit person. I am sad, I am confused with my life. But I have a path to follow. And I know that if I can resist the temptation to do bad habits, and replace my life with neutral and good habits, my life will become better. That's all. My neutral and good habits include hitting the gym, reading and writing, preparing for exams, sleeping well, making time for sketch, dance, digital art, acrylic painting, being good at my work, and treating people with respect.

I am glad that I am one week into not doing bad habits. I am happier and more conscious in my life. And, it has been beautiful because I am not a better person.

Da Malemnganba, da Lamjingba, da Nelson has been a good example in my life. They are doing well in life. Because they are good humans. And, they deserve to be in a good position in life. They gave me hope. I followed them and set out a foundation in my life. Maybe that's one of the reasons why when I remember them today, I smile. When I remember them in their formal dress during their Farewell Party, I smile. Yes, all I did was smile back at them. I didn't say thank you. I didn't say, "Thank you Da Lamjingba for everything. Thank you for your time as a senior and helping me during the speech. Thank you for allowing me to spend time with you and meet da Malemnganba. All these seemingly simple but impactful events shaped my life."

18 December 2025 Thursday

I think that I need to talk to Prabir Laishram, a fictional character from a Manipuri novel, Khudam Ama.

Me: Hi!

Prabir: Hey, how are you?

Me: Not good. I am on a boyfriend crisis. Need I say more? You already know what is happening with my life. Can you help me?

Prabir: (smiles) Dear Arun, I am all aware of whatever is happening in your life. There are good things happening, and not so good things happening as well. Good thing is you have got the back of Natasha, Sanjana in your life. Bad thing is you are still doing the bad habits. I know you want to change, but just speaking about it will not help. You need to take action.

Me: I do know that.

Prabir: Then what is stopping you? See! You cannot keep on blaming Patrick. He is also a human and he has his own limitations. You are in charge of your life. Do you want this life? Or somewhat better?

Me: I want to improve my life.

Prabir: And how can you improve your life?

Me: Loving Patrick without any expectations, focussing on my career, health and well-being. I need to be disciplined in my life, sleep regularly, think good about my life.

Prabir: Good! For now, love Patrick, there are no restrictions in loving him. But, as said by Natasha, the ball is in his court. From your end, it's clear that you stand for this relationship. It is from his end whether he will stay in this relationship or not. Also, don't be too much irritating, annoying to him. Just let him be. He is going through alot. You are also going through alot. But, I know you will take the right decision starting today. Please don't relapse into bad habits. Arun, I have many hopes from you, become a top-class writer, top-class dancer, top-class civil engineer.

Me: Okay!

Prabir: You have so much potential. You need to start valuing your time. Patrick should not be the centre of your life. Your ambition for self-improvement should be the centre of your life. And, you should work on that. Whether Patrick stays in your life, or doesn't stay in your life, should not matter much. I know it's better said than done, but we cannot deny the possibilities that your relationship with Patrick might end soon. Your relationship is aligned more on the negative outcome. So, you better be prepared and careful if Patrick leaves you.

Me: Actually, I have made many mistakes in this relationship. I cannot and shouldn't do things that can cost me this relationship. In fact, I should do things which align with my future goals.

Prabir: Tell me your future goals.

Me: Be a good husband to my husband, be a good civil engineer, be a good writer, be a good dancer, be a good artist.

Prabir: You have many faults at present- you use dating apps even while you are in a monogamous relationship, you don't study for civil engineering exams, you don't hit the gym regularly, you don't eat healthy foods, you don't diet well enough, you don't make time for your hobbies. Yes, you do give time for writing, and I appreciate that. But, you can do so much more. Let's not blame the world, Patrick for your own shortcomings. I believe in you Arun. You can do so much better.

Me: Prabir, it's so easy to speak all of this. But it's not easy to do it.

Prabir: Fine then, let's take a six day challenge. 26 December 2025 is the last day. You have seven days in your hand. Change yourself. Love Patrick as much as you can, but also hit the gym, dance, read, sleep, pray. Don't think till 26 December 2025 whether your relationship with Patrick will work or not. Give all your problems and issues to God. For now, your goal is gym, diet, dance, sketch, writing, civil engineering and proper sleep.

Me: Okay!

Prabir: Update me everyday! Also, could you please focus on Waheigi Leiteng? Your deadline is coming soon, and you are crying over Patrick. Remember, life will go on, but your 20s will not come back again. Spend your time wisely. And, take care of yourself. Update me anytime, I am always available for you.

Me: Thanks Prabir, you too, take care of yourself.

Prabir: Thanks Mr Author.

Let me be honest here. I love Patrick so so much. But, presently, the scenario is not in my favour. He is able to not call me for a week straight. And when I call him, he doesn't pick up. I also had multiple outbursts of blocking and unblocking him. I think we have built resentments in our relationship. My mistake is that I am more anxious in this relationship. I fear that he will leave me. I fear that my life will be led as a single person, without any partner. For me, he is not just my boyfriend, he is my identity. I want a man who can stand for me and proudly call me his boyfriend. But, for now, he is not that person. He is ashamed of himself. He even doesn't want me to use his name in my own biography.

I have started to feel that this is not worth it. Instead, I should devote my time on tasks such as preparing for civil engineering entrance examinations, gym, writing, reading, keeping myself busy with hobbies. Only then, I can make something out of my life. As said by Prabir, I have a target to complete the manuscript 'Waheigi Leiteng.'

I texted Patrick, "I am planning to cook Ooti and fish fry for you tomorrow. You can have that for dinner when you come home. Don't worry, I am not going to stay."

He replied back after ten minutes, "No thanks."

I got a sudden feeling which was a combination of sadness, anger and disappointment. I texted him, "Has your resentment build this much that you don't want to connect with me? Are you planning to end our relationship? Please don't leave me."

I texted him a few more sentences, "Do you wish to have some alone time? Why are you not interested in me anymore? Why are you doing this to me? Why is this happening? You are coming to Bangalore after a month. This could have been a happy moment for both of us."

My brain knows that I have been treated like shit. My brain knows that I should leave him. My brain knows that I should focus on more important things in life. But, somewhere, my brain also replays those happy memories with him. In fact, I am staying in the rent in Marathahalli, where we both used to stay. I will be returning to the rent in Medahalli tomorrow as he doesn't want to meet me. It's sad because I thought of meeting him. It's sad because I thought I could hug him, cuddle with him, have some intimate moments with him. On the contrary, he doesn't want any of that. In fact, he doesn't even connect with me.

A person who can go without contacts with his parents for a month, can go contactless with anyone in his life. He can even leave me. I love him. But I also know his potential and it's really threatening. He is not dependent on me, I am dependent on him emotionally. He should not be my only source of happiness. I made a mistake by making him the centre of my life. I cannot focus on my studies, hobbies, gym, writing, and learning languages. Somewhere along the line, I have lost contact with myself. Is it better to let go of this relationship?

I cannot answer this at the moment. Fine, even if it gets over, there will be record of how I felt. I want to curse him. I want to curse him so badly. But I shouldn't. I should respect him. I have made enough mistakes in the past. I cannot repeat the same mistakes again. There should be respect in a relationship. There should be mutual understanding in a relationship. And if it isn't there, then it's better to quit the relationship. Because there's more to life than this relationship.

I have made a pact with myself. I swore on my career and my writing that I will break up with him if he doesn't contact me within the next 200 hours. I should have written 100 hours, but I wanted to give him a more better chance. And in those 200 hours, I am not supposed to install dating apps, watch porn, masturbate, use Instagram. It's kind of a detox for me. Rajeev is also a stimulus. I hope that after these 200 hours are over, I am arrived with more clarity and understanding about my life.

I should end this relationship with him because he is emotionally unavailable. And he will never change, I need to accept him the way he is. But my heart beats fast, I have a sensation of heartburn because of him. And it's very unhealthy in the long run. I hope that I choose myself along the journey. He chose his parents. His mom told him, "Try to make distance between you and Arun. Try to forget him, slowly, day-by-day." How am I supposed to respect my mother-in-law who speaks of breaking our relationship?

She had hopes that her only son will be married to a woman. She dreamt that she will also be a grandmother to her grandchildren. If Patrick was born straight, it could have been possible. But, he is gay. He is into men. And, it will be a suicide for him if he marries a woman under family pressure. I know everyone is hurting. Patrick is hurting, his father is taking antidepressants, his mother is in hypertension. And I am crying to him to save this relationship. I understand him, but there's a pain in me. And the pain is, he didn't choose me. I wasn't his priority. Even now, he doesn't text me asking how I am doing. And this means, he has moved on. Love may be there, but his actions make me feel very less important in this relationship.

21 December 2025 00:37 AM

The day which was supposed to be a happy day has turned into a gloomy day. Future is definitely unpredictable. I have already texted Patrick a multiple times. I think letting him go is the best solution for now. But as Natasha said, "Don't jump into conclusion for now and take the concrete decision." I really love him but why he is doing like this to me. Why is he not giving time to me? Why is he not caring for me? Why is he silent? Why does he not care about this relationship?

I cannot deny the fact that our relationship is on the verge of getting over. For whatever reasons, maybe it is because of my multiple partnered nature, or it is because of his emotional unavailability, the question that arises is will I still choose him if given the choice? 'Yes, I will' is the answer I have in my mind. We both are so different. I am an expressive human, he is a silent human. It really hurts. I hope he solves all the problem and mysteries.

At this hour, our relationship not working is more evident. Why am I saying this? From his end, the communication is getting scarcier. I am not able to keep up with this behaviour. I don't know what to do. I don't know how to keep up. What will I do if this relationship doesn't work?

I will be crying like crazy. I will feel as if my future is crashed down upon me. I have had such a beautiful future planned with him. And he opted to choose his homophobic bestfriend, parents over me. Or, am I just blabbering while he is seeking for more time to process things? He could have just said that he needs time to process things. Also, why am I only blaming him? I have also so much on my plate. I need to make good use of my time, no matter what. Whether he stays in my life, or he doesn't stay in my life, I should focus on my physical and mental health, education, career and hobbies. One of the reason why I am vulnerable to him is because I think I am not enough for him. And he never says, "Arun, you are enough for me. And, I am there for you." Is it too much to ask from a partner?

I know the situation is intense. Both of us belong from a relatively homophobic society. He is the only son in the family. His father is sick. He is surrounded by homophobic friends. His mother disapproves of our relationship and constantly reminds her son to end our relationship. And, he is also not happy in this relationship. He must be feeling that I am dragging this relationship. It's time to stop being angry. It's time to take care of myself. It's time to observe.

As Natasha said, "Remember Patrick, you are not leaving this relationship. What you will be doing in the coming few days is sit and observe. You will need to quietly observe what is happening. He might call you for Christmas, Emoinu, New Year celebration." I am hurt. I am hurt of his treatment when he is in stress. Why does he not count on me when he is in stress? Why did he ghost me? Why is he ghosting me? Why is he saying that he needs some alone time, instead of meeting me and finding a way? It's his right. He can do whatever he pleases. And, that's important to understand that amidst all this crisis, I have to prepare for my future.

If he doesn't prioritise me, why should I prioritise him? Why am I prioritising him? I have so many things to work on. Maybe this is a sign from the universe that I should now divert my attention to other important things. It's my fault that I have made Patrick the centre of my life, whether I like it or not. He is lucky that he got someone like me who loved him this deeply. And he has taken me for granted.

Future is unpredictable. But, I can make things in my favour. To be honest, each day is precious. Each day is an opportunity to work on each other. It is our loss that we are letting days to pass by, and make distance between us. It is true for my career as well. If I study everyday, I will end up somewhere better. If I write everyday, I will end up writing a complete manuscript someday. That's call consistency.

Oh Patrick! I love you so much. You will never understand. Oh Patrick! If you could love me back as much as I love you.. Oh Patrick! If you can handle all this situation pretty well.. Oh Patrick! If you can save me from all this stress.. Oh Patrick! I feel as if you have given up in this relationship.. Your silence kills me. Your silent nature hurts me alot. Why are you like this?

Can I just slap myself? Can I just slap myself for always talking about him? Can I just slap myself for still holding on to this relationship even when it is quite evident that it is about to end? Ufff! It hurts like crazy. I remember the poems that I wrote while in pain. And also, this manuscript that I am writing, it's all written while I am in pain. I think this is the price we pay for being an adult. Life goes on no matter what. I think I must not overthink about this anymore. "Come what may," this is what he said. He didn't say, "I will save this relationship. Don't worry Arun, I will convince my parents. I will stand by you."

It was me who said, "Patrick, just survive. I will take care of everything."

Well! Then I should take care of everything. I should give my best to save this relationship. Will I be able to do this? Communication is key. Time will come when we will communicate. It's so hard not to talk to him. That's what love is - hard, sad, toxic where I forget all other things in life.

What about my father? Does he have any idea about my relationship? What matters is my identity. What matters is my choices I make in life. What matters is my character. I need to work on myself. I need to be busy and do the needful. I choose my sexual orientation as my utmost identity. I am proud of my roots, culture, and also my sexual orientation. If I had to say this, I would say, "Papa, I love you. But I also love myself. I cannot hate myself for being a gay man. I am having a hard time Papa. A guy whom I deeply love is not treating me well. But, in real life, how do I explain this to you? You are 72 years old, and I am concerned of your health too. What will happen if you get shocked with this news? That doesn't mean I am not proud of myself. There are many things where I am not proud of myself. I am not loyal to my boyfriend. I don't study as much as you think I do. I am an average guy with average skills for now. But I was born to touch the stars. I think that I have sacrificed a lot of myself to a guy who doesn't even care about me."

Is taking care of myself that hard? Are inculcating good habits which align with my future goals that hard? I need to make a life where Patrick is not involved. Because that will be my back up. I am definitely in grief. I am definitely in pain. I am definitely speechless. But I have hope.

I summon upon Prabir again.

Prabir: Arun, will you for once stop contacting Patrick for three days straight. All I am asking is stop texting him, calling him till 24th December, 2025. If he invites you for Christmas Celebration, you should go. Do what Natasha said, love him, don't leave him, but observe him from a distance for now. Also, your life is not just about Patrick. He is important, no doubt. But, you also have a bunch of syllabus to complete, office work to do, he doesn't pay your bills, you do. Also, don't do husband job at boyfriend's salary.

Me: I also know that it's better if I don't connect with Patrick for now. But, I am not able to control this.

Prabir: You want him to change, but you yourself are not changing. This is how hard it is! Either you love him the way he is, or change yourself before telling him to change.

Me: That's so true! And yet, very hard to follow.

Prabir: Where is that topper Arun who was studious, ambitious, goal-oriented, optimistic? I miss that Arun. I know you must be thinking that I am a fictional character, and why I am complaining about you. But, since you seeked my advice, as a friend, I would suggest you to be busy with your life. This is grief. You are in grief. I am sorry for you. I am sad for you. But you have to walk through this path alone for now. I am there. I am just one thought away. But, you are supposed to walk this path alone. Remember, it's better to walk alone than with an emotionally unavailable person who drains your energy.

Me: Do you want me to end this relationship?

Prabir: No, not for now. Because I know you will be hurt if you do that. All I am saying is follow Natasha and Dr Geeta's advice, give him the space. There will be a time for confrontation as well. But for now, you are very vulnerable. And trust me, no one wants a vulnerable partner, when he himself is going through alot. Be like a self-reliant person, don't bother him. Take care of yourself, he will take care of himself. Oh Patrick! You are about to be 27, and this is how you treat yourself.

Me: I am not drinking alcohol. I agree that I am crying inside, but I also know what's best for me.

Prabir: Oh really? Then why did you stress eat the other night? Why did you not care about your health? Why are you stressing over Patrick too much? Why are you not indulging yourself in solving RRB JE MCQs. Remember Arun, you are no longer a kid anymore. Love is important, but so is career, life, hobby, health, overall well-being. You need to take care of yourself. You need to love yourself. You need to respect yourself and step away from the relationship, if this is what your self-respect demands.

Me: I understand Prabir. I will try to be better.

Prabir: You better take care of yourself. You are no less than anyone. You are a published author, you are a civil engineer. And you also know where you are lacking. You lack in emotional stability. You are as vulnerable as a volatile gas. And that's what makes you more emotionally rich. That's what makes you more of a writer than a civil engineer. See, there's also a life beyond Patrick. I want you to know that. And, you have very limited time on this Earth. Value your time, and everything will fall in place. It's not always about productivity, it's about happiness, fulfillment and making choices you won't regret in life.

Me: Thank you Prabir. Thank you for believing in me. Thank you for guiding me when I need it the most.

Prabir: Now go, live your life. You owe Patrick nothing. You have already done your part. You now have to focus on other things. Remember, whether he contacts you or not, it's beyong your control. So it's better you do things which are on your control. Don't worry too much, life goes on. You worry on only one topic, where in fact, you should worry about your career, hobbies, goals, and self-improvement. Patrick is dragging you and keeping you away from being your best version, but love is not materialistic. So, I am not going to say that you should kick him out of your life. Just be careful, he is not a good husband material.

Me: I love him so much.

Prabir: I know Arun, my sweet Arun, I know! You love him, but does he love you? Does he love you enough that he will provide a stable life for you? I don't think so. I don't think so because the way he is acting now, this is very toxic. He should not go silent when you need assurance. He should not become emotionally unavailable when all you need is emotional connection. It's as if you are begging for this relationship. Why do you have to beg for a relationship? It has to come naturally.

You need to work on yourself. Forget Patrick for a while, focus on gym, diet, proper sleep, novel writing, novel reading, civil engineering, mental peace and self-improvement. Value time. That's all Arun, that's all for now.

Me: Okay!

I cry a little thinking about the conversation between Prabir and me. He is not wrong. I have been giving too much attention to Patrick that I couldn't give time on my career. Good memories with him flashes back again. But there are bad memories too. Today is a bad memory. He doesn't want me to meet him today. And it's hard for me to admit that I have lost a gem.

What about the hidden gem inside me? I have not taken care of myself lately. I should study, read, write, sleep well, think positive, and do the needful. I need to stay away from Patrick, he is negative, very negative energy. Deep inside, I want Patrick to come back to me. Let time decide whatever it is. And, the need of the hour is not worrying about him, rather I should worry about my health. I need to give him space.

What can I learn from my school life? I had a heartbreak too. But I am at peace with that heartbreak now. That means, I can survive this heartbreak too. I have realised one thing in life, Patrick does not value me for now. The thing is he is not in his best version. And, that means, he is having a hard time. It is best for me to give him time. Rather than asking myself why he is not giving me time and attention, I should divert my attention on my career, hobby and life. Only then I can do something good in my life. I am happy that I realised it at the end.

Oh dear Patrick, 21/12/2025 could have been such a happy day where I would have waited for you at the Airport, where we could have come back together, had quality time with each other. But you chose to stay alone. I respect that. I will not take any decision now. All I need to understand is his pattern. He is reacting this way when he is stressed. I should take note of it. And it is his character. This will be repeated in the future too. And if I choose to stay with him, this pattern will show up again. Will I still be angry at him for choosing to stay alone? Or should I understand him and shower my love? Time will tell. But for now, I need to take care of myself.

All my other factors had come to a halt. Civil Engineering theory studies have taken a pause, gym has taken a pause, novel reading has taken a pause, dance has taken a pause. Is this good? NO. Definitely not. Patrick is important, but I need to move on. He was good, I admit that. But for now, he is poison. And I should stay away from him until he detoxifies himself. I should restrain myself from texting him, contacting him. It is for the better. I do have a life other than Patrick. It is like we are going to break up. I think I need to break up with him. In a month's time, the answer will be well clear. Let's see where life takes me.

I loved him so much, and he turned out to be a coward. He turned out to be someone who cannot stand for this relationship. I am not going to blame him anymore. Let it be! Let it be! Let it be!

I am grateful that I am still in contacts with da Malemnganba. A few days beck, he texted me saying, "Are you in Manipur?"

I replied, "No da Malemnganba, I am in Bengaluru."

"If you were in Manipur, I would have personally come at your home to give you the invitation. I am getting married in January."

"This is indeed a very happy news da Malemnganba. Lamnganba told me. I am planning to come to your wedding.

But, I am not sure because the flight tickets are high. If I am not able to afford the tickets, I will not be able to make it."

"It's absolutely okay Arun. I am sending you a digital invitation."

It was beautiful. The invitation was printed on a golden paper. It was written in English with a beautiful cursive alphabetical design.

How did I end up like this? Being in so much love with Patrick. And he is not even picking up the call. I think he will end this relationship. I am saying this because he is not replying to my texts since a week now. He is less bothered about me. I will be okay!

I need to focus on my career and life. Those good memories with him resurface again. But I do miss him. My friend Anita called me a while ago. I told her, "I don't feel valued in this relationship. He said he doesn't want to meet me. He doesn't care about my existence. I think I should move on."

Anita replied back, "Let's not jump into any conclusion for now. Let's try to take things slow and focus on taking care of yourself."

"I will hit the gym, study for exams, dance, sketch, read more books, keep myself busy."

"That's the spirit Arun, I know you can do it. I want the studious Arun back. I want the better version of you back. You can come back to your best potential."

The thing about having friends is they support you when you are at your worst. I am not happy with my life because of this relationship. So, why don't I just keep this relationship a little away for now? Why don't I stop thinking about it for now? Why don't I focus on other things? To be honest, I am waiting for this one call from him. That one call saying, "Arun, I am back again. I love you!" This is how much I love him.

What did I learn from my school life? I learnt that books helps us no matter what. I learnt that books provide us with knowledge and security in life. I have lost contacts with books, maybe I should befriend books again. I should respect my time. I should respect myself. I should respect Patrick. I should respect his decision to be alone for a while. I should respect his decision to be detached from me. He has not spoken to me since a week. He has not called me. He has texted me in a very irritated manner. Why am I disrespecting myself?

..

Alright! Alright! Alright! I am at the Airport now. It's 06:38 PM and Patrick is arriving at 07:50 PM. How did this happen?

Around 1:00 PM, I called him. He hung up the call. I got sad again. But, he called me back about fifteen minutes later. All my anger, disappointments vanished when he called me. Just to listen to his voice hits me with dopamine. Yes! There are still questions inside me- Will our relationship work? Will he fight for our relationship? Will he stand by me? I don't want to ask these questions for now. I reminded myself of something, "Ball is in his court, there is no point in asking all these questions. From my end, I want this relationship to work. So, I will love him as much as possible while it lasts."

"Hello!" I said. I smiled when he called me.

"Hi! I am at the Kolkata Airport Lounge. It's bigger than the Guwahati one."

"Can I still come to pick you up from the Airport?" I asked in a calmer tone.

"Yes you may!" He replied back.

"Is your mood alright now?"

"I don't know. I have been having mood swings." He said in somewhat guilty tone. He seemed he was not proud of how he handled things.

"Yes, you have not been talking to me well for nearly a week now." I cannot deny the fact that he can survive without contacting me for a week. And, I am the one who will keep on texting him again and again.

"Can I cook Ooti and Fish fry for you? You are going to have dinner right?" I asked.

"I had plans to eat Hyderabadi Briyani for tonight."

"Let me cook dinner for you!"

"Okay!"

I was excited. Why shouldn't I be? A person whom I deeply love, with whom I haven't talked for more than a week has contacted me. But does he love me? Or is he lonely and just wants some time with me? I told myself, "Let's not be negative here. Let's focus on him."

So, I rode my bike from Medahalli to Marathahalli. Tears fell from my eyes while I was riding the bike. I was finally able to meet him. I bought Pork meat, visited North east shop and got garlic chives, sawtooth corriander, king chillies, pumpkin, mustard leaves. I had initially planned to cook ooti and fish fry, but changed the plans. It was 3:00 PM when I reached the rented room. I cooked rice, boiled pumpkin and mustard leaves, and pork curry. I didn't know if Patrick will like them or not. The pork curry was abit spicy because of the king chilli.

There is pain inside me that I am unable to express fully for now. Why did Patrick not contact me? Why did he stay silent for over a week? Why did he not call me, text me, connect with me? Well, on the positive side, I got to know his reaction when he is in stress. He tends to shut himself out when he is in stress.

I need to accept this version of him if I want to continue this relationship. Also, I need to focus on my health, life, career and hobbies. I am doing quite well in my life. I am happy. He has given me enough dopamine for today to get me going.

What is special about Patrick that I love him so much? He is different. He is good. He is attractive in his own ways. As a gay man, there are already very few gay men who will ever agree for living as a couple. He told his mom, "Mom, I am planning to spend my life with Arun. I will take care of you, I will take care of dad, but please don't meddle in other affairs, including this one."

Many things happened after this, I blocked him thrice, he stopped texting me back, I unfollowed him on Instagram, and there has been many sad instances as well. But there shouldn't be any ego in a relationship. My love for him clearly outweighs the pain that comes with it. I am thankful to God that he listened to me. I am thankful because I had submitted all my prayers to him. I had told God, "Dear God, I submit this case to you. It has become out of my control. Patrick is coming to Bangalore and he doesn't want to meet me. It was supposed to be a happy day, and it ended up being sad. I am scared, I am sad. But I need to take care of myself too."

God has listened to my prayers. I have one more wish, "Dear God, please protect my relationship with Patrick. I want to spend my life with him. I want to grow old with him. I want to be with him. I think of no one except him. I cannot live without him. I know, it's toxic that he has become the centre of my life. And I love him more than he loves me. But I cannot help it. I really love him."

Other problems become small when he is with me. A school boy who was timid, scared, hiding his sexual orientation has now become a lover, Mr Gay India 2025 first runner up, writer, dancer, artist, and an engineer. I have gained a lot of identity capitals along the way. And I will continue doing so as well. For now, as I wait for Rajeev at the Airport, all I can do is smile, embrace this moment. I am happy. I need to stop being anxious about my future. I need to live in the present. And the present is really good.

The clouds have settled for a while. I don't know when it will surround me again. The cloud of fear, uncertainty, hopelessness will grip me again. But, for now, the sunrays of hope has hit my face. And I am happy. I have hope. I have a possibility which is excited to tell me, "See Arun, everything is going to be okay. Patrick is back in your life. Hold on to him, don't leave him, for he is your hope. He is the love of your life. He is your everything."

As I see people with their luggages, people of multiple ethnicities walking over at the airport, I can only realise that each of them has a story within them. My story is all about Patrick, my evolution as an individual, all the experiences which has shaped me to what I am. It is about accepting my flaws, and trying to change them, improve them for a better version. And I think I am going in the right direction. I dare not trade Patrick with anything.

And I think I am happier.

I am planning to write a few short stories.

Chapter 2

Is this even possible?

I sat down to write a short story, taking inspiration from my own life. The title of the short story is - Is this even possible?

“Are you serious?” Kelvin asked.

“Yes, I am.” Parikshit replied back.

“Raising a PIL at the Supreme Court is a very big task, it will cost you a lot of money. Do you have the money?”

“I know of only one thing, and that is, if I don’t do it now, it will be too late.”

Parikshit is planning to raise a PIL at the honourable Supreme Court. He wants same-sex marriage rights to be recognised in India.

“Now that you have decided, I cannot stop you.”

Parikshit thinks that now is the right time to take action in life. “I am scared. I am not sure what the outcome will be. But this needs to be done.” He tells himself.

Parikshit has a boyfriend. His name is Laksh. They have been together for five years now. Not all partners are the same. Parikshit is more open about the relationship. He wants to introduce Laksh as his boyfriend to the world. But, Laksh has issues. Laksh is the only son in the family. And he has been facing parental pressure to get married to a woman.

"If I had the same sex marriage rights protecting me, I would not have faced this situation. Is my relationship with Laksh any less than a heterosexual relationship? Is my love for him any less than a husband would love a wife? I don't have adoption rights. His family is threatening me. His best friend is telling me to sacrifice him for the sake of the family. This mentality has to change. I will bring the change." Parikshit tells himself.

Parikshit visits Advocate Samson. Samson has a big mansion in Iroishemba. Parikshit and Samson have studied from the same school, Maria Montessori School, Imphal. Samson is from the batch of 2011, and Parikshit is from the batch of 2016.

In the front of the mansion is a garden, where a round white table is placed. It is the beginning of winter. And it's quite a good time to soak the winter sun, while having morning tea.

"Do you think raising a PIL is an easy task? You need to be well clear about what you are looking for? It cannot be just Parikshit Maisnam v/s Union of India. You need to prepare well," said Advocate Samson.

"I have come to you with a purpose. I strongly feel that you will guide me. As my school senior and an elder brother, please help me," Parikshit pleaded.

"Parikshit, I too believe in same-sex marriage rights. I am also well aware about you and Laksh. Laksh, being the only son in the family, is facing marriage pressure. And you think that only judicial intervention can save you. Am I right?" Samson asked.

"Da Samson, I have always admired you since my school days. I was in Class VI, when I first met you. I need your guidance here. My relationship with Laksh is no less than any heterosexual relationship. It needs to be recognised, otherwise, the parental pressure and the heteronormative society will make it hard for us to survive. To be honest, I feel depressed, hopeless at times because of this societal pressure. Deep down I know that it is a negative thought. I need to start somewhere. And it's the first step."

"Okay Parikshit, I will help you in all possible way. I will not sugarcoat this, let me be very clear, this is going to be a tough journey. I will do everything possible to help you."

"Thank you da Samson."

"Maria Montessori School turns 40 this year. Are you not planning to visit our school?" Samson asked.

"I have also been thinking. I think I will be going."

"Great! We can go together then."

Most of the batch of 2011 opted their career in computer engineering. It was a trend. Only a handful of seniors chose different fields, Samson was one of them.

Laksh is stressed. On one side is the family pressure, and on the other side is his identity. Laksh is really unsure about his life. His father has a chronic disease which needs surgery. He blames himself for hurting his parents. He blames his sexual orientation for his life scenario. His mother wants him to get married to a woman. But, things got uglier when his parents came to know about Parikshit and Laksh. Parikshit, on the other hand, is in a dilemma. He loves Laksh so much. But, he is somehow tired of this battle. The plot is awesome, no doubt about that. Two men are in love with each other. One man loves the other man more. The other man who loves less is attacked by external factors of family pressure, drama, leading him into a state of indecisiveness and confusion.

Parikshit would question himself, "Why is he acting this way? Why is he so emotionally distant? Why doesn't he call me back? Why does he ignore my calls and messages?" The answers are unclear. However, in this scenario, it is very evident that their relationship is in a fragile state. It can come back stronger, or diminish into a no relationship. Laksh cannot choose between his parents and his life partner. He cannot choose because he wants both of them. But he is ashamed of himself at the same time. He loves Parikshit but the very concept of a gay relationship disgusts him. This is why Laksh is not responding to Parikshit's texts and calls.

Parikshit is determined to save this relationship. He knows that life would be hard without Laksh. Yes, it's hurting when Laksh doesn't respond to his texts and calls. Parikshits tells himself,"I feel like I am ignored, unseen, invisible. But I love him. All I can do is love him, work on myself, and wait for the right time. It's not that Laksh has left me yet. He has his father and mother to take care of. Being an only son has its own price, and he is paying the price. I love him, and I will do what can be done in my capacity."

Parikshit thinks deeply and tries to find out a way forward. "I don't want any gay man who wishes to marry a man go through what I am going through. Had there been sensitisation, had there been same-sex marriage rights, had their been acceptance in the society, I would not have faced these problems which I am facing presently. My in-laws would have readily accepted me or at least I would have had a legal stand to save my relationship. There wouldn't have been any grudges between Laksh and me. Resentments have started to build up. I have this fear whether the relationship will survive or not. But I have hope. I have my schoolmates, school seniors and juniors to whom I can seek support."

Parikshit met with Samson often. Samson suggested, "Parikshit, you should start an online campaign where you sensitise the people, as well as raise funds for your PIL. It's high time you do that. Also, read about the NALSA judgement, Navtej Singh Johar v/s Union of India judgement, history of LGBTQ+ equality struggle in India. I know it's hard to state that legal recognition of same-sex marriage rights is in the hand of Parliament, not on Judiciary, but we will try."

Parikshit read about the NALSA judgement, and researched about the LGBTQ+ history in India. It was a mind widening experience.

Parikshit asks himself, "Is it even worth it? Is it even worth it to fight for someone who doesn't care anymore? Is it worth the energy?" He feels as if he is losing the battle. Some relationships work, some doesn't. "I have started to feel that I am the only person putting efforts in this relationship. But, it's rewarding to listen to his voice, see him smile. I forget all my worries when I am with him." And there comes the ultimate thing, "I accept him the way he is. Presently, he is silent, emotionally unavailable, doesn't support me, and is rather living life unbothered. But I love him. And he is lucky to have me. Things have been hard for him. It's still hard, yet we have not called off this relationship. It is in fact a chance to focus on myself, choose my growth, amidst all the chaos. I can come back better. I am born to be a leader, it's time that I deviate from my follower mindset, and follow on my leader mindset. Also, it's not only about him. It's about me and my identity. And I deserve respect whether I am born gay or straight or bisexual."

Samson and Parikshit went to the 40th Annual Day celebration of Maria Montessori School, Imphal. The stage was beautifully set. It was nostalgic for Parikshit to visit the school after a gap of four years. "I have completed 9 years post my Class XII exams." The Physics lab, Biology lab, the Welkin Block,

Basketball court, football ground, badminton court gave him a rush of memories. "This Physics lab was the very place where I met my best friend," "Basketball court and it's craze during in-house competitions," "My first crush who turned out to be a straight man and the heartbreak after that, hahaha!" "My speech where I got stuck in the middle," "Farewell pictures," "The school honour boards and the names of the school toppers written there," all reminded him of his memories in the school.

Samson was the topper of his batch, the batch of 2011. Samson is different. He pursued BA LLB after Class XII, even though he had taken up science in Class XI and Class XII. There's a saying that goes, "Being present and showing up is important." Parikshit showed up in the 40th Annual Day celebration and it opened doors for him. Samson had already set up a dinner with fellow Marians, from diverse batches and backgrounds. Some were teachers, some were engineers, some were doctors, some were writers. It was crucial to have an Alumni unofficial meet, for Parikshit.

The dinner was arranged at the Classic Grande hotel. The beautiful warm lights gave a warm and welcoming ambience. 30 Ex-Marians joined the dinner. Samson had already planned this since a week before. Parikshit was also the second topper of the batch of 2016. He was short of 1 mark each from being the subject topper in every subject. That's okay as it made him more famous in school, as the second topper who was one mark less than the topper's. He scored 94.8%, one mark short of getting 95%.

"Dear Ex-Marians, we are gathered here tonight to support Parikshit. Parikshit is planning to raise a PIL for recognising same-sex marriage rights in India. But, we know the present scenario, it is also in the hands of the Parliament to make this ultimate change. I am doing my part in helping him file the petition, guiding him for fundraising, and like today, we are increasing the visibility of LGBTQ+ individuals in the country."

They are gathered at a round table. Samson gave this welcome cum agenda speech.

Robin, from the batch of 2013 said, "We are here to help you Parikshit. Samson has already told us about your PIL filing process. We will help you. To begin with, I have a suggestion. Why don't we plan a meeting with our honourable Lok Sabha MP? If we could convince him, things will be better."

"To the point," said Vaishali. "But how do we meet him?"

Robin smiled and said, "He happens to be my maternal uncle's best friend. I can arrange a meeting."

"Great!" said Samson. He continued, "I am also concerned about the fundraising for the PIL. Can we contribute some amount from the Alumni fund we have?"

"That's a good idea," Tampha said. She was from the batch of 2018 and knew Parikshit as her senior. She continued, "I will check the funds and confirm. But I feel we can go with 5 Lakh rupees for now."

Parikshit was grateful to receive this monetary support from his peers. "Thank you everyone," he said.

"This will give us the resources to start the legal battle at the court. We have a long way to go Parikshit." Samson said with a smile.

"Sure da Samson, I am all in." Parikshit said. He felt grateful for being supported by his school seniors, juniors and classmates.

Meeting with Dr Neelamani, Honourable Member of Parliament from Inner-Manipur Lok Sabha constituency was scheduled. Robin, Samson, and Parikshit went to meet him at his residence in Mantripukhri.

Dr Neelamani Ngangom was a college professor at University of Delhi. He was elected from the National Liberal Party, which is an opposition party. Elections are due on 2029. Chances are slim that he will be considering this request. There are issues of the social conflict in Manipur, internally displaced persons have not been able to visit their homes since May 2023. There are issues of insurgency, unemployment, halt in railway projects due to general strikes. He has many things on his plate already.

"We have an appointment with Dr Neelamani. Could you please contact with the personal secretary?" Samson told the security guard, who was sitting near the gate.

"Sure sir. Sir, kindly do your entries on the register," said the security guard, giving the register to Samson.

Security guard talked with the personal secretary. They were soon allowed entry to the Building. The house was a three-storey building, painted in white. There was a Shree Govindaji Temple near the main gate.

They entered the meeting room which was located in the first floor. Robin made this meeting possible. He requested his maternal uncle to convince Dr Neelamani to meet them.

Dr Neelamani was a wise man, in his late 50s. His personality was that of a wise educated man, whom this country genuinely needs at the moment. He came to meet them with an open mind. He was wearing a white polo shirt and a oak white formal pant. On top of the polo shirt, he wore a light grey coloured jacket, which matched his grey hairs. He was also wearing a pair of spectacles, which made him look more approachable.

Samson, Robin and Parikshit stood up as soon as Dr Neelamani arrived.

"Please be seated," Dr Neelamani said.

"Good Morning sir," Samson said.

"Good Morning, would you like to have tea or coffee?" asked Dr Neelamani.

"Coffee!" said Samson.

"Tomba, four coffees please!" said Dr Neelamani. He smiled at Robin and said, "Hello Robin, your uncle Tompok told me that you wanted to meet me, is there anything I can help you with?"

"Uncle, I have a topic to discuss. It's about introducing same-sex marriage rights bill in the Parliament. Parikshit, is my school junior, and he is a very ambitious man. He is working as a Engineer in Bengaluru, and he identifies himself as gay. He is facing challenges from his in-laws, and he feels that it's right time that same-sex marriage rights bill is introduced in the Parliament."

Dr Neelamani thinks for a while, and replies, "As a member of National Liberal Party, I believe in creating a liberal space for every community, regardless of their gender, religion, caste, etc. I do believe as well that same-sex marriage rights should be given. But, there will also be people who will be against this, and it may affect our vote bank. Manipur is still conservative. And as you mentioned, his in-laws are against his relationship with a man. I am sure there are many people who will be against it."

"Sir, is there no chance that we can work on this? It doesn't have to happen overnight. I am also preparing to file a petition at the honourable Supreme Court in the coming month." said Samson.

"I will need to talk with the spokesperson, leaders from the Party. One good thing is that LGBTQ+ equality rights are part of our party's manifesto. And we will be working on it. I do see hope. I am from the opposition party, and it's hard to pass a bill from the recommendation of an opposition party.

But, it's still better to do something than doing nothing. I will do the needful," said Dr Neelamani.

"Thank you sir," said Parikshit.

"You can call me uncle Neelamani," Dr Neelamani said with a smile. He continued, "Parikshit, you are lucky to have good friends in your life. They are supporting you in your tough time, and you will need more of their support in the coming times. How old are you?"

"I am 26."

"26 is a very young age. I hope your marriage with your boyfriend is legally recognised in the coming years. I will do the needful from my end."

Things are tough. Parikshit is scared. He is unsure about his relationship with Laksh. He is hopeful though. He is hopeful that things will be in his favour. He is hopeful that the relationship with Laksh will bloom again. And he will marry Laksh, legally recognised by the Government of India.

Three months down the line, things are turning a little better. Relationship with Parikshit and Laksh has become stable. As it is rightly said, fights and disagreements are important to grow a relationship. They have come back stronger. Laksh has decided to keep his relationship lowkey for now, considering his parents' health conditions. His parents doesn't approve of this relationship and he doesn't want to get into more complexities. But he is doing his part as a boyfriend too. He is showing up in Parikshit's life by celebrating their anniversary, valentine's day, planning Parikshit's birthday, congratulating him on his new book.

Parikshit has also made peace with Laksh's behavior. He did feel as if he was a dirty secret when Laksh decided to hide his relationship. But, he realised that in the present scenario, this is the best decision. Too much public exposure can ruin a relationship, especially a gay relationship, as there will be more hate comments than the positive ones. And, he wants relationship with Laksh to last a lifetime. So, he compromised in this matter. Apart from that, he is doing great. He has filed a petition before the court. Samson is helping him through the process. He is going to Delhi the next month for the hearing.

“Hope for the LGBTQ+ community,” reads the Headline in the India Xpress newspaper. Honourable Inner-Manipur Lok Sabha MP, Dr Neelamani Ngangom urged the social welfare minister to look into the implementation of same-sex marriage rights in India. He emphasised on the importance of these rights in bringing equality for the LGBTQ+ community. “LGBTQ+ population in our country is estimated to be about 10% of the total country’s population. And it is high time for us, as a legislator, to care for them, consider their demands and make India a more liberal country. I, on behalf of National Liberal Party, urge the government to consider the same-sex marriage rights. We cannot just wait for the judiciary to act. We, as responsible law makers, should consider the pleas of the LGBTQ+ community,” said Dr Neelamani in the Parliament.

Parikshit smiles as he reads this article. He tells himself, “There is hope!”

Isn’t it easy to develop a story? In real life, what Parikshit did, is hardly possible. This is why I love fiction. I can change the scenario, circumstances, and turn things in my favour. Laksh and Patrick are in the same scenario. Parikshit and I are in the same scenario. Parikshit chose to fight for his dignity. I will too. I don’t have the money. I don’t have the resources presently. But I will do start somewhere. I think I have already started. This book is a testament of what a gay man feels in India.

There are moments where I want to end my life. I am being very negative here. I do have hope in my life. But I also do have suicidal thoughts coming up sometimes. As I am writing this, the birds are singing. It's about to be sunrise. I again tell myself, "There are so many things to be happy about. I am working at my dream company, which celebrates LGBTQ+ identity. I am working in my dream city, where I always want to live. I am working and also making time for writing, which is one of the important skills I have. I have so many reasons to be happy."

I am sad because life as a gay man in India is not easy. Either I hide my sexual identity and live an anonymous life, or live a fake life as a straight man, only then I can escape this fear. But I don't want to. And that's where the struggle begins. I don't have the energy to fight with the heteronormative society everyday. I do have my near and dear ones as well in this society who care for me. If there are people who hate me for my sexual identity, there are also people who accept me for the way I am. And I should remember that I am in 2026. I am 27 years old and I am a youth of this country. As a youth of this Nation, I do have a say in what is happening in this country. I will fight for my dignity, my rights. I will work on myself to be a better version. I will work on myself to accept that this is going to be hard, but this path will make the life of LGBTQ+ individuals in the future. This is what hope is. We work for the future.

Why did I date Patrick? I dated him because I thought I have a future with him. And it is not going how I thought it should be. And that means, there is uncertainty in future as well. That's what makes life wonderful. There should not be uncertainty as well. I know that I am in pain, I am hurt, but I will get over it. He didn't stand for me to save this relationship. Unlike the short story, where Parikshit fights the world to save this relationship, I will give Laksh the opportunity to fight for this relationship. If roles were reversed and if Laksh were told to save this relationship, he wouldn't have. He has rage spiral.

Rage spiral is a new term for me. Patrick has better English vocabulary than me. And it was him who told me, "He is on a rage spiral." I checked the meaning on wikipedia and that's when I realised the true meaning of this term. Why is there shame, self-loathing, guilt in us? Why is being gay so hard to accept? This is again a lesson of self-acceptance. We need to accept ourselves. We need to love ourselves, only then we can love others.

I ask myself, "Arun, what did I learn from this short story?" I learnt that I have a long way to go. I learnt that I should not blame Patrick for this failing relationship. I learnt that I should care for things which are in my control, and not care for things which are outside my control. I learnt that I should have hope in life. I learnt that I should invest in people who invest in me. I learnt that I should forgive myself.

Chapter 3

The Blue Lotus

I write another short story named – The Blue Lotus.

It is a full moon day. The sky is clear. Stars are twinkling, and the autumn winds are creating a soothing feel. In the midst of the Loktak lake, surrounded by the Phumdis, are Geeta and Sanathoi.

"Sanathoi, I am here to reveal you a secret. The reason why we are meeting here is for a reason," says Geeta.

They are sitting on a wooden boat. There is a warmlight emitting LED lamp illuminating the boat.

"I missed you mom," Sanathoi says

"I missed you too son," Geeta continues. "You have grown up now. I wish I could spend more time with you."

"Are you happy?" Sanathoi asks.

"I am happy. I am happy to see you grow son. I am here for a reason. It's about the blue lotus."

"The blue lotus?" Sanathoi asks in a surprised way.

"Yes, the blue lotus. It grows in the Loktak lake. One can find pink lotus in plenty, but this blue lotus is rare. I want you to find the blue lotus, care for it and keep it with you for life. You can consider this as my gift to you."

Sanathoi wakes up. "The blue lotus," he can still hear the words his mother said. By coincidence, today is full moon day. And his mother also came in his dreams on a full moon day.

Sanathoi is a hardworking person. He is a quality estimation engineer in a private company in Imphal. His mom passed away a year ago. Usually, he would wake up, hit the gym, eat breakfast and head for office. But today, things are different. He woke up with a dream in mind. Some dreams lingers for quite some time. This is one of them. "Why did my mom mention about the blue lotus?" He asks himself.

He hits the gym, but this question pops up again. He decides to go to the Loktak lake and see for himself. He comes back to his home and tells his father, "Papa, I am leaving for Loktak lake. I will be coming tomorrow."

Sanajaoba didn't stop him. He calmly says, "Travel safely and call me once you reach there." Sanajaoba wants to ask some questions such as, "How many of you are going? Where is it?" But he wants his son to take his own decisions, so he doesn't ask him.

"Okay Papa"

Sanathoi takes out his Royal Enfield and sets out for Moirang. He contacts a homestay in the Loktak lake, named Changkhonbi homestay. Tompok, the owner of the homestay says, "You can stay, of course. We will pick you up from the Sendra boat station."

"Can I also have a boat for myself during the night?"

"I will try. It is not advisable considering the risks, because it will be dark, and there might be unwanted incidents." Tompok says.

Sanathoi understood what the term unwanted incidents meant. In a conflict torn region like Manipur, insurgency creates fear. Tompok continues, " If something happens to you, the reputation of our homestay will be at stake."

"You have a valid point, I understand. It's a sincere request because I need to find something. I take the full responsibility for any consequences."

"Okay then, I will provide you with a boat."

Sanathoi parks the bike at the Sendra Boat station. Tompok comes to pick him up. There are other people too – a family of four, a gang of six of college going students, and two foreigners, and three solo travellers. They are a total of sixteen people. Sanathoi is assigned a single sharing tent. It is amazing. The tent is placed on wooden plank above the phumdi, surrounded by the Loktak lake.

Dinner is served at 8:00 pm. After dinner, Sanathoi goes to the tent and takes his diary out.

Dear mom,

You came in my dream today. And I am here in the midst of the Loktak lake. I am searching for the blue lotus which you told me to search for. Bless me mom with your guidance, for I will need you. I hope I get the peace I am looking for. I hope I get the purpose in life I am looking for.

Your son,

Sanathoi

As requested by Sanathoi, Tompok gives him a boat. "It is a full moon day, so there won't be complete darkness. But, be careful. The water is cold. Call me when you need any help." Tompok says.

"Okay!"

Sanathoi sets out sailing the wooden boat. He has an LED Lamp with him, and a torch with him as well. And he starts to search for the blue lotus. There is a portion in the lake where lotus grows in plenty. People make handicrafts out of the fibres of the lotus stem, hence the lotuses are a source of income to the local villagers. He enters the portion and starts searching for the blue lotus.

"Mom, I hope that I find the blue lotus," he tells himself. As he is searching for the blue lotus, a man in his mid 20s speaks to him, "What are you looking for?"

Sanathoi is surprised as he hears someone talk to him out of nowhere. "I am looking for something, a blue lotus."

"Blue lotus? Haven't found any blue lotus yet in my life." The other guy is also on his solo boat.

"It's rare. I am looking for this rare lotus." Sanathoi says.

"What's your name?" the mysterious person asks.

"I am Sanathoi from Thangmeiband. And you?"

"I am Rajeev, but people call me Neelkamal as well."

"Neelkamal is the translation of the blue lotus." Sanathoi tells himself. "Hello Rajeev, nice to meet you."

"Hello Sanathoi, nice to meet you too. Let's search for the blue lotus you are speaking about."

"Sure!" Sanathoi tells himself, "My mom said the blue lotus is a gift from her. And I should keep it with me. Is Rajeev a gift from my mom?"

"I think I have found the blue lotus," Sanathoi says as they are searching for the blue lotus.

"Where? Where is it?" Rajeev asks curiously.

"But you will not believe my story!" Sanathoi says.

"If you don't tell me, how can I decide whether to believe it or not?"

"Okay," Sanathoi says and continues, "My mom came in my dream today. And she said that blue lotus is a gift from her to me. And..."

"And?"

Sanathoi continues, "I am feeling that you are the gift my mom was talking about. Your name is Rajeev, which is a synonym to Neelkamal, the blue lotus. Is it just coincidence or is this what my mom wants?"

Rajeev smiles and says, "I believe your story Sanathoi. Did your mom say anything else?"

"My mom said to care for and keep the blue lotus with me for life. I know in the context of two men, this sounds too gay, but this is what my mom said."

"Quite interesting, to be honest, I think this is beyond our control. This moment, how I ended up here at the right time, when you are searching for the blue lotus, and you telling me your dream, it does make sense." Rajeev continues with a smile, "We can be friends, if you don't mind."

"Yes, sure!" Sanathoi says with a smile.

Some people come in our lives as magic, just like a surprise.

"Which homestay are you staying in?" asks Sanathoi.

"Thoibi Homestay, and you?"

"Changkhonbi Homestay"

“Come let’s sail for a bit and talk about life,” Rajeev suggests.

Both of them sail through the Loktak lake. The moonlight is bright enough to distinguish the phumdis and the water, and they are sailing. The cool breeze is soothing.

“I like dancing in bollywood songs. But I am afraid to upload in youtube because I might get negative comments. And that is stopping me from uploading the videos.” Sanathoi says.

“We all have fears in one way or the other. I fear water, I fear swimming. But I am here sailing with you in the Loktak lake.”

“How are you managing your fear?”

“You cannot see what the other side of the story is, unless you overcome the present story. There are possibilies that you can get negative comments, but there is also an equal possibility that you can be liked by people. You are unique in your own way, and you should follow your passion.”

“Okay!”

Rajeev poses himself as the King and speaks in a commanding tone, “I, your blue lotus, command you to post youtube videos of your dance starting this week.”

“Hahaha!” Sanathoi laughs.

“Hahaha!” Rajeev joins him as well in the laugh.

“Okay, my Lord!” Sanathoi says bending his head.

They talk for a while, about life, friends, family, passion, hobbies, plans in life. Sanathoi feels happy that he met a friend out of nowhere.

“Where are you from Rajeev?”

“I am from Moirang. I am a full time traveller, and I make vlogs as well.” He winks and says, “I can help you with the editing.”

"Okay!" Sanathoi asks, "What were you doing here?"

"Since when I was a kid, I had always wanted to sail through the Loktak lake. The weather was also very supportive today, with a clear sky and a full moon. So, I decided to sail over here. And, I met you, in the middle of the night, using a torch and searching for something."

"Oh! That's good to know."

"I am leaving for Phuket tomorrow. I have a flight to board tomorrow afternoon."

"How many baggage do you have?"

"Just one carry on baggage," Rajeev asks playfully, "Is there any reason you asking me this question?"

"Um.. Do you mind if I drop you tomorrow to the airport? I have my bike."

"That's seems like a very good plan. At what time are you leaving for Imphal?"

"Is 8:00 AM fine?"

Rajeev looks at the phone, it's 01:30 AM. "We better get some sleep then."

"Yes!"

They exchange their phone numbers and sail to their respective homestays.

In the tent, Sanathoi opens up his diary and starts writing.

Dear mom,

I think I have found the blue lotus. He came out of nowhere, it's so surprising mom! I am happier. Thank you for bringing me happiness in my life. I loved the gift.

Your son,

Sanathoi

Sanathoi smiles and sleeps.

He leaves the homestay at 6:30 AM and reaches the Sendra boat station at 7:00 AM. By 8:00 AM, Rajeev is also ready at the Moirang market. Sanathoi drops him at the airport.

A new chapter has unfolded in Sanathoi's life.

They reached the Airport in an hour. At the departure gate, they talk for a moment.

"We will catch up soon," Rajeev says.

"Sure!"

"Give me your instagram ID," Rajeev says, as he checks his flight tickets and passport.

"Sanathoi123"

"Okay!" Rajeev follows his account.

'Rajeevthetraveller followed you on Instagram,' a notification pops up on Sanathoi's phone.

"Yup, that's me!" Rajeev says and smiles.

A new story unfolds. A story of hope, friendship, companionship, and love.

I smile when I read this short story. It is a sweet story of a budding love. And it reminds me of Patrick. I have so many happy memories with him. I wish if things were in the favour of our relationship. I cannot believe that our relationship is about to end. Actually, it has ended. I am just denying that it has not ended. There are evidences that this relationship is dead. He doesn't text me back. He doesn't call me. He doesn't ask me about my day. We don't stay together.

In a relationship, proximity, time spent, and energy are very important. We used to live together. That means proximity was there. We spent time together, the second point is also clear. What we are facing is the energy level. My energy level is adventurous at the moment. I want to explore the world with him, imagine a happy life with him. I choose him as my first priority. While his energy level is he is self-loathing. He blames himself for his parents' ailing condition. He blames himself for being the lone son who is gay and cannot give an heir to the family. God save me from this dilemma. I am back on my hurt phase again.

I will recover. I cannot keep crying and making my health deteriorate. In my life, Patrick is a poison for now. He may become a life saving elixir, I pray that he becomes that. But for now, understanding my health, my mind, and my emotions, I am sure that he is not right for me.

I wish I could go back to my school days and seek help from Natasha. I can always do that now as well. She has already given her verdict, "The ball is in his court now. He will be the deciding factor whether this relationship will survive or not. You are fully committed to this relationship. Don't think of Patrick as a red flag, think of him as a neutral flag. Think of him as a hobby, which makes you feel good when you give him time. Try not to expect anything from him. And yes, also don't invest too much energy on him, let's focus on saving your energy and using it somewhere else where you get more outcomes in your favour. As I said, sit and observe. Don't leave him, you don't have to leave him. Just sit and observe, calmly. You will get your answer whether to continue this relationship in a few months."

There are things which I cannot control. I cannot control Patrick's rage spiral. I cannot control Patrick's emotional response to me. I cannot control Patrick's decision whether to stay in this relationship or not. But I have also things which are in my control. I can stay away from my bad habits. I can take care of myself. I can accept the decision that comes along the way for this relationship. I need to choose myself first. It is my ultimate responsibility to take care of myself. And if taking care of myself means to end the relationship with Patrick, so be it. I will end the relationship with Patrick.

What are the things at stake? An imagined future palace breaking into pieces. I imagined a happy life with him. I imagined a small house in the countryside, with dogs and cats, watching the sunset, with Patrick beside me. And as of now, it doesn't seem to be possible. It is still possible, but the probable outcome is more on the negative side. I have done my best from my part, to the extent that I got mental stress, fatigue and emotional breakdown. I give up. I cannot do more than this. It is now Patrick's turn to save this relationship. I cannot give more energy, time and resources to this relationship anymore. It has crossed my ultimate threshold capacity of what I can offer.

Keeping negative things aside, I wish to remember good aspects of him. I wish to remember only the good aspects of him for now. My phone storage is 128 GB, and it was about 126 GB full. So, I decided to delete some data from my phone. And when I checked my phone gallery, I found memorable photos of Patrick and me. I smiled and felt better. I have been feeling sad, helpless about this relationship. I tell myself, "So what if this relationship ends, it was beautiful. So what if this relationship ends, there was love between us. So what if I loved him more than he loved me, we both loved each other. He gave me my first kiss. He was the first to whom I had a belief that I have a future with a guy. It might end now, but I cannot deny the fact that he was my first relationship, actual relationship."

I am such a crybaby. I am not the first man in this world to go through a heartbreak. I am not alone. And, I have bought four books that I will be reading soon enough to deal with this heartbreak. This is called self-repair. Just like a river cleaning itself through her self-cleaning velocity, I am also on a self-repair journey now. I will drink enough water. I will go hit the gym. I will read books. I will prepare for exams. I will do my office work to my best potential. I will write diary. I will give time for my hobbies. I will take care of myself. I know that it is easier said than done, but I can atleast try.

My friend Anita calls me. She has been a friend who would connect with me once a week. She tells me, "Don't get me wrong Arun. I want Patrick to be out of your life. I don't like the way he treats you. I don't like the way he abandoned you when he went to Imphal. You may not feel good now, but it's better to stop talking to him until he reaches out to you. And I am sure that he will not reach out to you."

"I think I will follow your advice. Why should I always be the person who keeps the relationship alive? He is not the Patrick I fell in love with. He has changed. And I know that change is inevitable, but he has changed in a negative way. I cannot hurt myself anymore." I am sad as I am saying this. There is pain inside of me. There is a part of me negotiating with me that Patrick will come back to me. But, I do know that if he had to change in a positive way, he could have changed by now. He didn't. He hasn't. And he is not changing. He doesn't care about me. How am I supposed to be in a relationship with someone who doesn't care about me?

Let's not live in the past. Let's not live in the future. Let's live in the present. The present is hurting. It is hurting. And, I think it will keep on hurting me for a few days now. I need to take a stand for myself. I will confront him about his behaviour in the coming future. I will ask him, "What am I in your life?" I will tell him, "I want you to treat me better. I want you to communicate with me. I want you to share what you are feeling. I want us to be best friends." I need to have the courage to move on from this relationship if he cannot provide me with stability, and hope of a beautiful future.

Life during school and college is a chunk of semesters and syllabus, with a deadline. After college, life seems to have no deadline at all. Everyone is on a different pace. My colleague has a son who is about two years old. And his life is moving on a different pace as compared to mine. My life is all about heartbreak, coping up with the heartbreak, pain, dealing with unsaid words to Papa, books, work life etc. for now. Each of us are on a different pace. My Papa is on a different pace than mine. My friends Natasha, Mala, Anita are on a different pace. And they all have obstacles in their lives. I am not alone who is facing the pain.

I am also waiting for my blue lotus. I do think Patrick is my blue lotus. But I cannot deny the pain he is bringing in my life. Is the pain worth it? I don't know. I deserve to be happy. I deserve to smile more often. It is my mistake that I gave Patrick the key to my happiness.

"I decide to keep myself happy. I hold myself responsible for my emotions. I hold myself responsible for my health. I hold myself responsible for my financial decisions. I hold myself responsible for my future." I tell myself.

Malemnganba's wedding is in two weeks. This book started as a tribute to his contribution in my life. And, I let my words flow. The words led me to realise about my life decisions. I realised that I am in grief, I am in pain. I ask myself, "Does da Malemnganba also feel pain? Did he also have any heartbreak in his life?" I don't have the answer for that. All I know is, he told me once, "Be clever, vigilant, and hardworking." I am not sure if I have any of these three qualities at the moment. But I follow him. He is my leader, and I am his follower. I will be clever, vigilant, and hardworking. I will not be able to attend his wedding as I am in Bengaluru and I had not booked my flight ticket to Imphal. But, he will remain special in my life. Always!

I remember a moment from my school life. And I want to share it.

"You did well Arun," Lamjingba said.

"Thank you," I replied back.

Lamjingba was the assembly conductor for Einstein House. And that day was a wednesday. There was a roster system among houses. That week was Einstein house's roster. While I was in Class XI, it was always Lamjingba, as much as I can remember, who would be the assembly conductor. I remember Lamjingba coming close to the mic and saying, "School savdhan, school vishram, school savdhan. Let's pray!" And the school prayer would follow. After the school prayer, the school song would be sung. We would be told, "Vishram," and the day events like news updates, thought of the day would follow. If Ma'am Principal or Ma'am Director had to speak anything, they would speak after the thought of the day. On wednesday, one student from the house is assigned to speak. That day, it was me.

I spoke on, "Importance of Higher Education in India." I started well, but I got stuck in the middle. I had to open the note that I had prepared and complete my speech. Lamjingba motivated me even when I got stuck in the middle of the assembly. One of the reasons I fell in love with him was his kind nature. As a 15 year old, we don't really know what love means. It's a happy feeling. I felt good, butterflies were on my stomach whenever I saw him. So, I conclude with this emotional evidence that I fell in love with him.

Looking back, I realise that I got stuck in the middle of the assembly thrice. I was given many chances. I spoke on International Literacy Day. I spoke on Head Boy Nomination day, and I was one of the nominees. I got stuck in the middle on these two events as well. I was given a chance to speak as a Class XII student in their final week of school life. I spoke well that well. I spoke well on the Farewell day as well. With each performance, I got better.

One of my classmates whom I like to mention is Waikhom Ganga. She was the House Captain of Einstein House. Maria Montessori School had a system that if a boy is selected as a House Captain, a girl will be selected as a House Vice Captain. I saw that out of the four houses during my Class XI, three House Captains were girls, and one was a boy. That shows that girls were more in the leadership authority than boys in our batch.

I was told that Newton House and Darwin House were the biggest competitors for the best house trophy. But under Ganga's leadership and Lamjingba's guidance, Einstein House created a history that year. And the performance of house during the foundation week was a deciding factor.

The foundation week 2014 was a festival for me. It will always remain special in my life. It was the week when I got to spend time with Lamjingba. During the foundation week, four houses compete for the Best House trophy. Einstein House has rarely won the Best House trophy. It was a beautiful week with all sorts of co-curricular activities. There was football, basketball, badminton, table tennis, carrom, shotput, 400 m race, 200 m race, 100 m race, etc. as part of sports. There was march pass parade as well which had one of the highest marks in the mark tally. In terms of literary work, there was poetry competition, best speech in the assembly, best news reader, best thought of the day prize as well.

I was overweight, underconfident and a relatively silent person. My personality shifted from a smiling, bubbly and welcoming person to a silent, fearful, too self-conscious person. In my head, there were questions which used to kill my confidence. Thanks to adolesence, I had discovered I am attracted towards the same sex. And I was so confused because my friends were attracted towards the opposite sex. "What will people say if they find out I am girly? Why am I girly? Why am I like this? Why do people make fun of my overweight size? Why am I attracted to men?" And amidst all this chaos inside my head, I found Lamjingba, a kind senior who presented himself as a beacon of hope in my life. I chose to stay near to him, because I felt safe near with. I felt good to be with him. He is a very kind person. During the foundation week, starting from the school assembly till the very last minute, I would stay with him.

During the foundation week, we wore our school track suits, along with our House shirt. The assembly, which had lines of students on the basis of classes before, was lined up in terms of houses. And that is why, during the assembly line up, Lamjingba and I were on the same line.

I still remember the first time I met da Malemnganba. It was for a choir group song sung by Class XI and Class XII students. He was among the students selected from Class XII. I didn't get to talk to him that day. I got the chance to talk to him on the foundation week. It was the badminton tournament. "Meet Malemnganba, my best friend," Lamjingba introduced him to me. Malemnganba has been clinching Gold Medal for badminton since two years. Lamjingba was also there representing the Einstein House. I was there to cheer Lamjingba during the match.

Malemnganba represented Newton House. And he got the Gold medal for Badminton. Lamjingba got the Silver Medal for Einstein House.

Natasha has always been a studious and hardworking person. From the moment I saw her, I realised that she has the caring personality. In POLARIS orientation programme, there were sessions. The programme was about building confidence in life, learning soft-skills like public speaking, team work etc. We learnt through games. One of the game was such that a person is blindfolded and told to walk across randomly scattered paper balls without stepping on them. The other person has to guide the blind folded person to walk across the path. Natasha was the other person. And that day, I realised that she has the ability to guide a person, and is a natural leader.

"Lift your right foot and place it about 50 cm to your northeast.. (the blindfolded person places the foot).. very good... then place your left foot about 200 cm to the north ... (the blindfolded person places the foot).. good." This was Natasha guided her friend in crossing the randomly scattered paperball route. No one else could complete the task. I also stepped on one of the paperballs when it was my turn.

I know Natasha as a kind and helpful person. During the Pre-Board exams in Class XII, I saw her study very hard for exams. She was sitting on other side of the classroom, and I was also on the other side of the classroom. Exams were in about an hour, and she was revising the notes. She doesn't give up till the last moment. I feel that I must have something good in my past life, that I got to have her as my best friend.

Chapter 4

The Final High School Year

The final year of high school was a mix of exam preparation and balancing school life. My day would start with two tuition classes in the morning, followed by school and two tuition classes in the evening. Some of my classmates had two tuition classes in the morning and two tuition classes in the evening. Thanks to this lifestyle, I got a pair of specs on my eyes by the time Class XII final exams were over.

I was not sure what to become in my life. I did tell my brother that I want to become a writer and a dancer. I want to dance in Kathak and become a writer. I feel that I have already achieved my goals. It's just that I have to upgrade myself with each passing year.

I am glad to be in contacts with Rasika, Ganga and Natasha. I am friends with my male classmates, but I feel more connected when I talk with my female classmates. Why is it so? I think it is my ability to connect more with the feminine energy than the masculine energy. Funny thing is I ended up doing one of the masculine profession, civil engineering.

Zoro wrote a poem. He showed me when I met him in Mysuru. Patrick and I went to Mysuru for a trip in April, 2025.

I chose this unattended loneliness that belongs to no one.

I try to deny the reality of why do I like someone who never answers back.

I hope you don't go too far away.

I didn't even wish for several things.

Just when you feel tired in life,

Come to my heart.

Rest for a while and I will make you a cup of warm tea.

Don't worry about me and please be as beautiful as you have always been.

Just like the flowers fall, I will live

With the joy of being hit by the wind.

I am amazed to read Zoro's poem. I was not able to grasp the true meaning of this poem when I read it first in Mysuru. Maybe that time, my brain had not tasted the pain of heartbreak. So I couldn't understand the pain behind this poem.

Before this heartbreak with Patrick, I never ever intended to read poems. But this time, poems hit me differently. It is indeed an emotion that touches our soul. This heartbreak caused me to feel more deeply. I have never been hurt this much in my life as much as I am now. Patrick, why are you like this? Why is your coping mechanism so different? Why do you have to go silent whenever things don't go your way? Why do you abandon me? Why do you make me feel unloved in this relationship?

To be honest, I have always looked out for the qualities of Lamnganba in every man I wanted as a partner in my life. It's funny that I end up being single. It's funny that I loved so deeply, still I ended up being alone in this world. I am 27 now. I have nearly four years of relationship with Patrick and this is what is happening. Seeing this relationship break, I feel lost.

I have never felt lost this way in my life. I always had a back-up plan in my life. I never needed a back-up plan actually. I did well with whatever came in my life. I know that I am not growing in my full potential speed, but I am growing in an averagely good speed. Here, in terms of relationship, I feel lost. I cannot say that my life would have been better if Patrick was not there in my life. He did well to improve my life. He got my account created in Naukri.com and LinkedIn. And, that way, I was able to get good offers in different companies.

I am getting the good memories with Patrick replayed on my head. I am hurt and I still long for the happy moments I spent with him. Is it going to be this hard for the rest of my life?

The problem is, what do I do now? Should I let this relationship die? If I don't do anything for this relationship, the relationship will anyway end. Patrick is not going to save this relationship. I have a friend who said, "The way you shower love to Patrick, I want you to shower that love to yourself. You have this inferiority complex in you that thinks you will not find anyone better than Patrick. You see yourself far less incapable as compared to Patrick. And, you are wrong. Arun, you are doing so much better in life. Learn to love yourself, prioritize yourself, and care for yourself as you want to care, love for Patrick."

It's not that easy. "In this hard time, you should try to socialize yourself. Instead, you are busy with office work, and writing. I know writing is expressing your thought out. But, you need to come out and do something for the community. The LGBTQ+ needs you. You are a little kid. But you will be fine. I promise. Puppy woofs you." When my friend told me this, I felt better. I am 27 and I think of myself as very old. But when he addressed me as a little kid, I felt better. I know 27 is a big age. It is an age where life decisions are made in a more matured manner. And here I am, crying over Patrick.

I mean I am crying over a man who can survive without talking to me for about a week. Fine, let me wait and watch. I will not initiate any calls, or texts this time. It's serious because I have to care about myself too. I cannot expect too much from him. He will not answer my calls. He doesn't want to connect with me. And, it is for my own good that I should also not connect with him as much as I can. Only then my dopamine will be under control and I will make better decisions in my life.

The final year of my school life has some important sections. I started to bond well with my classmates. Class XI was about understanding the school. Class XII was about living the school life. All the co-curricular activities were taken up by Class XI and Class IX. Class X and Class XII students were given the priority to study hard for the board exams. Amidst all this, there was a social unrest.

Tuition classes were also affected because of the conflict. Things got better after the month of September. Classes began to be held in full swing. I had one thing in mind when I was in Class XII, "I need to get 90% in my Board exams." I miss this Arun who was so much dedicated to his studies.

"I am planning to write a story on my school life," I texted Ganga.

"Wow! It's a wonderful news. I am looking forward to your book." Ganga texted me back.

My school life memories are incomplete without mentioning my Section C crush Zoro, school topper Arthur, Darwin House Captain of 2014, Reena, Section-D George and Benson. Section-D Sofia, Section-D Rasika, Section-A Calvin, the ILP struggle and the closing of school due to the social unrest.

I wanted to talk to Rasika, and I thought Ganga would be having her number. When I asked Ganga, she readily gave me Rasika's number. Sometimes all we need to do is ask. Reena Thongam was the class monitor of Section D in Class XI. In Class XII, it was Ganga. I was the other class monitor while in Class XI and Class XII. And both these years, I am grateful that they were the class monitors. I had less skills in fulfilling the class monitor duties. We had a bittersweet relation where I even got scolded from her for my less skills in managing the class monitor duties. No hard feelings as all of us were in our teenage years. One of the memories I have about Reena as a classmate was her reading of English novel during the class. I think it was a Physics class and the teacher had told us to solve a numerical problem. She had already solved the problem and she was using her extra time to read the novel.

During my school days, English scared me. I couldn't speak well, write well because I was underconfident. I would read a sentence but I couldn't grasp the meaning of the sentence fully. And there she was, reading a novel.

A profound memory I have of her is her smile at the Chemistry exam day at JNV Yaralpat. JNV Yaralpat was our examination centre for Class XII Board exams. She was on a van when she gestured with her hand asking how my exam went. I smiled the broadest smile I ever had and said it was good. I lied to her. The exam was not good. I tend to hide my sadness, consciously and subconsciously. And I got 72 out of 100 in Chemistry, which is a low mark because I wanted to get 80 at least. The point here is not my life, here the point is how I remember her. This was the last time I saw her in person. I never saw her in person after that.

Ganga shared me Rasika's number. I texted Rasika, "I was writing a book on my school life memories. And I thought of you while writing. Ganga gave me your number. So I thought to catch up with you."

"Hi Arun, it's really nice of you. How are you?" She texted me back.

"I am good." See! I lied to her again. I am dealing with my boyfriend's coping mechanism. But overall I am good, so it's not a complete lie either. 72 out of 100 is also a good mark and I should say that the Chemistry exam was good. I think I take my life too much seriously that I forget to enjoy the present. I did tell her some truth as well, "Feels good to catch up with you."

She replied, "Same here!"

"I wanted to know about you. Our Board exams at JNV Yaralpat was the last time I met you. I lost contact with you after that. What did you do after that? Benson would talk about you to me. You did BA in DM College, with him, that I know. Also, what are your best memories during your school life? And how do you remember me as a classmate?"

"Yes, Benson and I were collegemates. Presently, I am pursuing PhD at Department of History, Manipur University. The best memories I have is not specific. I would say, the moments I spent with my schoolmates were memorable. And about you, I remember you as someone who was bubbly, super outgoing and hardworking."

"Thank you so much Rasika." I smiled when I read her texts. Bubbly, super outgoing and hardworking. This is how she remembers me. I think I am searching for this version in me. I think this is why I am writing about my school life. I am seeking answers from my past, to help me in the present.

I cannot give up on my dreams. A few mistakes in my life cannot describe my character fully. I still have the chance to improve. I still have hope. I can be my hardworking version.

Actually, everyone of us are on different timelines. One got married last year, one is preparing for his PG exams, one is preparing for UPSC civil services exams, one has got into the Indian Army, one is doing PhD. A friend texted me saying he regrets to have wasted time during his college life, and he feels left behind. There's no single answer to success in life. I am actually living my dream. I have the money to buy my favourite pen, favourite novel, and I am not financially dependent on my parents anymore. It's just that I don't take care of myself enough. It's just that I put myself behind, and prioritize Patrick. And that's a lesson I learnt. I cannot and should not depend on a person to make me happy. It is my fault to think and expect that Patrick will make me happy. While, in fact, I should be in charge of my happiness.

My existence is precious. I am contributing to the Nation as a civil engineer. I am also fulfilling my soul through writing. I am considering to join Kathak classes soon.

Natasha and I are best friends. And I am grateful to have her in my life. She texted me, "How is your day going?"

I replied, "Thank you so much for asking Vy. I am having a breakdown, hehe! I am coping with it well though. Also, Waheigi Leiteng is in progress. I am making the final additions to this book."

"Vy you're strong! Still I'm just a click away if you want to text or talk. So, know that you're not alone." Yes, that's Natasha and that's why she is my best friend.

"Thank you Vy! I need to start loving myself more. I need to love myself the way I love Patrick."

"Yes, that's right. Love yourself and feel complete. He (you) deserve all the love and care too." Natasha said.

Self-care is not an option, it is a must. And I think I have realised that. The pain is still there, but not talking to Patrick makes me feel better. Actually, I have not cut ties with him. It's just that I have stopped initiating and contacting him first. He is free to call me, text me anytime. But he doesn't. He has ample time for uploading Instagram stories, playing video games as part of his coping mechanism. But he doesn't care to talk to me to deal with his problems. And that hurts me. That really hurts me. For now, not initiating to talk with him is a form of self-care. I need to take care of myself.

My mind is dependent of Patrick. I remember what I told Dr Geeta, "My life revolves around Patrick. I know I should not make Patrick the centre of my life. I should make my career as the centre of my life. But I am not able to help it."

"What you are experiencing is grief. You are thinking too much about your future and it is leading to anxiety. I want you to give space to Patrick. Why don't we think of it as an opportunity to work on your other goals? Don't initiate conversation with Patrick from your end. If he contacts you, reply to him. Can you do that?"

And here I am, not able to follow her advice. I am able to survive two days without talking to him. But I am not able to not contact him for a week straight. It hurts so much. I know he is going through alot. But, I am hurt because he does not share his thoughts with me.

Cognitive behavioural therapy is an exercise to break the loop of negative thoughts inside our head. Thought, emotion and behaviour are inter-connected. One must work on breaking the negative loop, otherwise the loop will cause more harm. I need to accept the reality. I need to accept the fact that I am at fault for not focussing on my career, and not accepting Patrick the way he is.

I tell myself, "I think I like my 27 years old self. I am able to distinguish what is good and what is bad. I am skilled enough to not take too much stress in life. I am living my dream writing this story. So, why don't I focus on things that make me genuinely happy, without depending on anyone?"

My life has meaning. I am meant to write stories. I am meant to become a better version. I will take care of myself. I will do the needful to make people happy around me. I need to be happy first. I need to love myself more.

When I talk about loving myself more, I remind myself of Zoro from Class XII-C, Einstein House. We both were class monitors of our respective sections. And there were instances where Section-C and Section-D students were merged because of less attendance. That is why, I got to have some connection with Section-C as well. Zoro was the carefree student of our batch. In my school life, this particular human has been special. I was the disciplined, obedient version who had an ambition to secure 90% marks in exams. I will not say that I made a bad decision choosing my ambition. But I did miss out on a lot of things. Zoro would bunk classes and play basketball during Section-B sports period. He would be the cheerful student, with a smile, who would also make fun of me for being overweight. And I was the touchy human, who would overthink everything. I would feel that he is making fun of my sexual identity. And, as a defence mechanism, I would be very rude to him.

Things got better after school. We became good friends. I told him about my insecurities, and he understood it. Actually, I did have a crush on him during my school days. I would look at him playing basketball, drenched in sweat, with his cheerful, slightly overloud behaviour, and it made me fall for him. I loved him. But there is also a thought. If our relationship were ever to happen, it would have already happened.

I am not seeking a romantic relationship from him now. All I have for him is respect, and friendship. I asked him, "Zoro, do you mind if I share your poem in my book?"

He said, "Yes, I am fine with everything."

A part of me wanted to say, "Fine with everything? Are you sure? I will then ask you to be my husband." I didn't tell him that. I need to stop looking for a life partner. I should invest on people who invest in me. Also, I need to take care of myself.

I do also have an opinion to share. This opinion is from Arthur. Arthur told me, "I am excited about your book Arun. But I do have an opinion to share with you. I don't really know if you have felt this, but when I came as a newcomer, I felt less accepted by the already existing students. I felt connected to you because you were also a newcomer, and somehow we shared the bond of an outsider."

I told him, "I can understand. Section-C had more oldcomers as compared to Section-D. In my section, there was a good combination of newcomers and already existing students, so I didn't feel that in my class. But yes, when Section-C and Section-D were merged, I did sense that polarity, but I was less concerned about that. I had you as a big competitor. I am happy that you are the school topper of our batch. I never hoped to be the school topper, but I am also happy with my performance." Apart from Class XII Board examination, I had not secured any rank. I was not even in the top 20 of my batch. That is when, in Class XII I gave my best shot and secured the fourth position. I earned that rank. I earned that position.

"You did well Arun. Also, you are the only student from our batch who writes novels. And I am proud of you."

"Thank you Arthur. I am proud of you too. Become the best version of yourself, I am already proud of you and your achievements. And I can say that you can do more." I told him.

He smiled and said, "I wish you the same Arun. Keep writing, we are waiting to read your work."

I don't remember who won the Best House trophy when I was in Class XII. It must have been either Darwin or Newton House. Since da Lamjingba was not there, and my attention was also on board exams, I couldn't give much attention to the sports, and literary events' results. I did take part in the events. I did take part in the cultural dance performance by Class XII students, and it was an amazing experience.

We did the dance practice sessions during the Foundation week. It was a beautiful memory. My dance partner was Reena, who happened to be the crush of Arthur. One funny thing is Arthur and Reena went to the same college. And they don't talk to each other. I am friends with both of them, so I would meet both of them. What actually happened was Arthur proposed Reena in Class XII. Reena didn't accept the proposal. They were from the same section too. And I felt that this must have created some awkwardness and distance between the two.

Reena and Arthur are now doctors. They are both preparing for PG exams. Zoro is also a doctor. Ganga, Natasha are preparing for civil services examinations.

I do want to talk to Sofia. And so I texted Rasika whether she has any contacts with Sofia. I checked Instagram and typed Sofia Khoisnam on the search bar. And she was there. I smiled when I saw her DP. She has 317 followers and 300 following, and her account is private. She has always been a little mysterious. She was from Newton House, the same house as Natasha. I don't know what is presently doing in her life.

Ganga used to call her, "Dear Sobhamani." I don't know but this particular nickname stayed in my mind till today.

I know her as a hardworking person who was intelligent, was more conscious than me during my school life. She reminds me of Priyanka Chopra Jonas, who on her biography wrote that she changed schools at an interval of 2-3 years. Sofia was also a newcomer and she certainly added more diversity to the section. I have a belief that when a student goes to a new school, he or she carries some part of the previous school along with him or her.

Benson was also a newcomer. Maybe that is why, I do remember him as well. He was different. I liked his straight forward, no nonsense way of talking. His previous school was Patrick's school too.

I would always say that Section-D was different because of my fellow classmates. Also, Section-D was introduced for the first time from our batch. And that's what makes Section-D special.

In the session 2014-2015, Einstein House won the Best House Trophy. I am happy that I was part of the Einstein House. It felt like a collective win because we did something which was rare. Our house won March Pass, literary events. We lost in basketball but were placed in second position. It was very uncertain until the last moment, and that's what made our win memorable. We tried no matter what.

Why am I looking back to my school memories now that I am in 2026? I am seeking an answer. I am seeking my hardworking version of me which I have lost somewhere. I need to ask myself what makes me happy. I need to stay away from habits which has negative impact in my life. I think Patrick has a negative impact in my life, at least at this present moment. And it's better to stay away from him for now. I am not seeking for an immediate answer about our relationship. I should live my life. I should make healthy choices. I should be happy. And I should take care of myself.

I can take care of myself through a healthy daily routine. My daily routine should be filled with tasks, and activities which energises me to live. I need hope in my life. I need happiness in my life. Dear Marians, we are all at our own timelines. You might also be going through a hard phase. As a fellow Marian, I wish you the very best in achieving your dreams. We should remember our motto: Deeds not words. Vive la Maria Montessori School, Imphal!

Chapter 5

Papa, bless me with a happily ever after!

Dear Papa,

I am scared to tell you that I am gay. I am worried about your health. I am worried about your reaction. I am worried about my life without you. Papa, save me from this pain. I fell in love with a man, he is 30, and I love him so much. I wish life could have been easier for me. But, it's hard. Being an adult is hard. Being a gay is hard.

But Papa, I have chosen to accept my identity. I love my sexual orientation now. And, I respect myself. I will not choose Patrick, you, or anyone first, but my identity. If I don't love myself, how can I love others? I hope you will understand the dilemma of your beloved son. I have regrets that I have led you down in some way. I cannot marry a woman, I am not meant to be in a heterosexual relationship. I am adamant that I want a man in my life. And that's final.

In terms of my career, I think I will continue pursuing my career in civil engineering. I think I will also contribute in writing, gym, learning Kannada, Tamil, Telugu, Malayalam in my lifetime. I think I can work on myself and be the best version. I think I will be pivotal in the journey of implementing same-sex marriage rights in India. I am scared, as a 26 year old man, I am scared.

My boyfriend said, "I will never be fully happy, in both the lives." What he meant to say is, he is not happy with his life. He cannot be happy in only choosing me, and in choosing his family too. He is not fully happy in both the ways. He has led his parents down, that's what he feels. And for me, the relationship is alive because I am sticking to him. I have already told my friends that I have broken up with him. But in reality, I am still sticking to him.

I cannot leave him. Let this love destroy me, but I cannot leave him. I just can't. He is my purpose in life. He is my biggest achievement. He is my cheerleader. He is my witness in my life. I know this is not a matured mind speaking. I have many other areas where I need to put my focus on.

But, I am in love with him. I need him in my life. And, until my last breath, I have chosen to stay with him, however hard it gets. I will stand for him, stand by him, love him, care for him, talk to him. Papa, I know you want my ultimate happiness in my life.

As your son, I seek your persmission to kindly give me the choice to choose my life partner. And I choose Patrick as my life partner. I choose Patrick because he is my first relationship. He is my first love with whom I have completed nearly four years of relationship. You may find it disgusting, as his parents felt that way, and you are also from that generation. But this is the reality. I cannot deny the fact that I love him so deeply. It's not his fault entirely too that he is scared of publicly accepting my relationship with him. He has also faced the harsh reality of the world. And it is heartbreaking.

His parents are getting older and weaker, and being the only son in the family, it becomes his responsibility to take care of them. "I have more presssing things to focus on in my life," he said. He didn't say, "Whatever happens, I will stand for you Arun." He didn't say, "I will protect you from the world." He is being realistic. He has no energy to take care of me. And, I agree with him. He needs to take care of himself first. I must say, I am scared of losing him. But, I am also happy that I know where this relationship stands.

This relationship will stand if I sacrifice more. It's not that he doesn't love me, it's just that I love him more. I love him way more than he loves me. And those who love more, are bound to feel more hurt. It's natural.

So, what do I do Papa? I love writing. I will keep on writing. I will keep on learning new things. I will keep on loving Patrick.

Papa, please bless me with a happy life. I pray for your good health.

Love you Papa!

Your son,
Arun

17 January 2026 Saturday 05:53 AM

Dear Papa,

I am hurt. I am in pain. Patrick has again become distant from me. He doesn't talk to me properly. And I am bothered again. I might act strong and say that I am not bothered. But in reality, I am bothered. I cannot breathe properly. I have developed stress in my life to the extent that I have fatigue. My clinical psychologist told me that I am in grief. For a dead person, I can be in grief. That's relatively easier than to be in grief for a living person, in my opinion. A part of me wishes to think that things will get better. My heart wishes my relationship with Patrick to get better. But why so much pain, and why only me who is facing this pain. It's very hard. I wish I could tell you all this in person, but I am not able to.

I am crying as I am typing this. I feel like a failure. I tried my best. I tried my best to save this relationship. I fought with my own insecurities, I fought with my fear, I fought in every possible way to save this relationship. And now, I am not able to. This is the best I could do, and I couldn't save it. Things are the same. I don't know if I will be in a relationship with him or not, but as of now, I am not happy. I am not happy how he is treating me. I am not happy with what he is going through. I am not happy with how he is dealing with his situation.

How can I be in a relationship with someone who hates himself? I feel lost Papa. I have so many pressure in life. Exam pressure is there as well. In the month of February, I have four exams coming up, and I have hardly prepared anything. I do have a job in Bengaluru, as a Civil Engineer. I should not be saying this, but I tend to think many negative things for now. I have a loop of negative thoughts in my mind. I fear what if I get kicked out of my job, because of my incompetency. I am not incompetent. I know that I will improve, and I will improve in my life.

I cannot keep blaming myself for things which are not in my control. I should not blame myself for this failing relationship with Patrick. It hurts, it hurts like crazy. I wanted this relationship to last. I wanted to set an example that I can be in a happy gay relationship. I think I am wrong. He is not the right person for me. Otherwise, I should not have felt this pain, this hopelessness in my life. Is he worth the pain? No. He is not worth this pain. I cannot be in a relationship with someone who cannot take care of himself.

Papa, I really wish if you could understand me. It is you to whom I talk daily. And it's hard to think that you will not accept me that way I am. And, I am not able to convince you as well. Why do I think that it is my job to convince everyone to accept me? It is actually not my job. And I am much more than my sexual orientation.

Through this letter, I tell myself that I am not in charge of Patrick's happiness. I am in charge of my own happiness. And I will follow my clinical psychologist's advice to not contact Patrick as much as I can. I don't know whether this relationship will last or not. This will most likely end. Because I can sense more pain than happiness in this relationship. He is a coward, he is a self-loathing person, in terms of accepting his sexual orientation. And I must let go, for my own peace of mind. Ufff! It's so hard. It's so hard.

I wish if I could predict what my 35 year old me would say to what I am feeling. I wish if my future me would come to me and say, "Things will get better over time Arun. You are healing. Remember that this is the most important period of your life. Live it, feel it, learn from it, and take wise decisions in life."

On the good side, I have accepted myself and my flaws. I choose to stay away from my negative habits. I have decided that I will devote my time as much as I can to books, hobbies, gym, and experiencing life. I should not invest on someone who doesn't invest in me. Patrick doesn't invest in me, I should not invest in him. I will follow what Natasha said, "Observe, stay calm and observe." I have realised that the coping mechanism of Patrick is not aligned with what I want from my life partner. He tends to shut himself down, ghost me, not discuss anything.

Papa, you tell me to study hard for my upcoming exams. I feel that I should focus on my career. Heartbreaks are part of life.

This is what makes us human. I will work on getting myself better. I will work on myself. I will kill my insecurities and be a more optimistic person. I cannot keep on crying over things I cannot control.

Your son,
Arun

Alright! Alright! Alright! I am not going to end this book on a sad note. Yes, I agree that I have a thing going on with Patrick at the moment. I would also like to bring to your notice that I have not been feeling well. I will be going for a medical health check-up soon, very soon. I will take care of myself. I will do the needful to be happy in my life. Patrick matters, but I matter more for myself.

But let's look at the positive side too. I am 27 now. Patrick was there to celebrate my 27th birthday. So, he is not entirely bad either. I am working towards a disciplined life. I have realised that I need a dopamine detox quite often. I have realised that I have to live each and every moment. Life is precious! And it's complety okay to feel what I am feeling – sad, happy, angry, disappointed, hopeful, etc. The emotions are what makes us human. And I think, I have made a good garland, the garland of words, of my life. I will see you all soon.

I am thankful that I have supportive friends like Natasha, Mala who helped me during my tough time. I need to take control of my life. It is high time.

Oh yes! I forgot to tell you why I cursed Patrick at the airport. It doesn't make much sense anyway. I was angry at him because he didn't console me after I caught him using the dating app. Don't judge us. It happens! I still love him no matter what. I have made so many mistakes in my life. But I don't think of Patrick as a mistake. He is my biggest achievement of my life.

I wish that I end up with Patrick. I wish that I become a happier version of myself. I wish that I become the better version. I wish that I become a very good writer with time.

Signing off,

Yours truly,

Arun Potsangbam (or I should say, Arun Patrick Konthoujam, husband of Patrick Konthoujam)

29 January, 2026 Thursday

"Arun, I was, I am, and I will always be yours. And you are mine. There's no denying that. Life has been hard for me, and I was not able to give you time. As our relationship turns four years, I wish us a Happy fourth Anniversary." Patrick tells me, looking at me. We are watching the sunset together from the Varkala beach, holding hands. I feel peace.

How did we end up here? Well, some things are meant to be kept secret. Hehe! I am happier. We mended our relationship. We escaped our mundane routine to make time for each other. I do have insecurities inside me. I do feel that once we return from the trip, he will become his emotionally less available version again. And I need to accept him the way he is.

I feel the teenage version is also happy for me. I am doing well in life.

I love him. I love myself too. The relationship is saved. I am focussing on my health, career and life. And, as of now, this is the happy ending.